Se[illegible]...
& Conflict

...Plus!

SNEAK PREVIEW OF
SECRETS... & CONFESSIONS

SOME SECRETS ARE JUST TOO GOOD TO KEEP TO YOURSELF!

Sugar Secrets...

Sugar
SECRETS...

...& Conflict

Mel Sparke

Collins
An imprint of HarperCollins*Publishers*

Published in Great Britain by Collins in 2000
Collins is an imprint of HarperCollins*Publishers* Ltd
77–85 Fulham Palace Road, Hammersmith, London W6 8JB

The HarperCollins website address is
www.**fireandwater**.com

9 8 7 6 5 4 3 2 1

Creative consultant: Karen McCombie

ISBN 0 00 675437 6

Printed and bound in Great Britain by
Caledonian International Book Manufacturing Ltd, Glasgow

CHAPTER 1

STOLEN KISSES

Kerry Bellamy peeked in the window of the End-of-the-Line café as she hurried along the rain-speckled pavement.

As far as she could make out, there were only two people inside the comfortingly steamy café on this dull Friday morning. One was a youngish, scruffyish guy, whose eyes were glued to the tabloid propped up in front of his plate. Over by the counter, oblivious to everything except the music he was listening to, Ollie Stanton hammered out a beat on an imaginary drum kit. Grinning to herself, Kerry hurried towards the door, hoping to catch him in mid-drumroll.

"Kez!" grinned Ollie in surprise as he gave a final, noisy, metallic clang to the coffee machine with a wooden spoon, in accompaniment to the end of the Fatboy Slim track playing on the small radio by the till.

The lone customer, who'd already jumped at the sudden tinkle of the bell above the door as Kerry came in, now leapt at Ollie's loud exclamation and at his amateur attempts at percussion.

"Careful you don't put a dent in that, Ol!" Kerry grinned at him, pointing to the large, rumbling coffee machine. "Or Nick'll put a dent in *you*!"

"True – but only if he catches me!" Ollie grinned back. "He's skiving off next door just now. Said he had to catch up on something at home while the café was quiet."

"So you're all on your ownsome?" Kerry commented, pulling a clown-sad face.

"Nearly. One breakfast-with-everything—" Ollie nodded over to the scruffy bloke, who was flicking through the sports pages while he shovelled a loaded forkful of beans into his mouth, "—and that's been it for the last hour. Business has been as quiet as... a very quiet thing."

Kerry settled herself on one of the stools along the counter and leant her chin on her hand.

"So is Nick still talking about taking a few days off next week?"

"Mmm," nodded Ollie, leaning both arms

down on the opposite side of the counter from his girlfriend. "He might as well – there's not enough work for all of us at the moment. And anyway, me and Anna always seem to have a right laugh whenever he leaves us to run the place by ourselves."

"Aren't you forgetting something?" Kerry pointed out mischievously.

"What's that then?" asked Ollie, blinking at her through his floppy, brown fringe.

"You two could never run the place without Dorothy and Irene!"

Ollie crinkled up his nose and smiled fondly at the mention of the two ex-dinner ladies who made up the rest of the End-of-the-Line café's hard-working staff. Both the old dears were totally besotted with Ollie's charm – he always managed to get them giggling when they shared shifts.

"Ah, my girls..." he sighed, holding both hands to his heart. "Actually, I've been meaning to ask them both a favour."

"Oh, yeah?" said Kerry, her eyes wide and disbelieving behind her specs. She could sense a joke coming.

"Yeah," Ollie nodded seriously. "I was thinking of asking them if they fancy doing a bit of go-go dancing at our next gig. You know, get them in white bikinis and white leather boots on either side of the stage. It could be a great gimmick, couldn't— *ooof*!"

Kerry had pulled off the damp tea towel he had draped over his shoulder and wrapped it round Ollie's face.

"OK! OK! They don't have to wear bikinis!" he protested, holding his hands up in surrender. "They could just wear shorts and boob tubes!"

"Oh, *you*!" giggled Kerry, wincing at the incongruous notion of the two grey-permed, sixty-something women swapping their aprons and M&S blouses for something so tacky.

Ollie ducked another swipe of the tea towel and then lunged forward to sneak a surprise kiss on Kerry's lips.

Immediately, she paused, her hand still floating in mid-air, cloth dangling, while her heart pitter-pattered at his touch. But as quickly as she melted into his kiss, Kerry broke away again.

"Ollie!" she said reproachfully, glancing over at the café's one customer.

"He hasn't noticed!" whispered Ollie. "Too busy catching up on the footie and stuffing his face!"

Still, Kerry felt a little awkward kissing in public like that, even if the only public that was around wasn't taking a blind bit of notice.

"So, the café's still feeling the squeeze with

the exams being on?" she asked, trying to smooth back her rebellious hair. One kiss from Ollie and her curls seemed to have sprung out of the hairclips that tried to restrain them.

"Yeah, everyone's too busy swotting and stressing to hang out here. Speaking of which – shouldn't you be at home playing around with highlighter pens and memorising facts you'll never need?"

Ollie had never been much into school and had been more than happy to leave as soon as he'd sat his GCSEs two summers ago. He knew he wanted to do something special with his life, even back then, but until he could figure out just what it might be, he'd agreed to help Nick out temporarily at the café, as well as at the second-hand record shop his uncle owned next door.

At the time, it had seemed to Ollie to be a better idea than staying on at school. Only trouble was, two years down the line, Ollie still hadn't sussed out what that something special could be and his job with Nick was looking a whole lot less temporary...

"Hmm, well, I guess I got a little stir-crazy, holed up in my cell. Sorry – my *room*," joked Kerry, nonetheless looking guilty for sneaking away from her studies. "And having those double-glazing workmen arrive today was bad news.

They've been hammering about the place since 8 o'clock, yanking out the old windows!"

"Talk about bad timing," said Ollie sympathetically. "Couldn't your folks have put them off till later?"

"They tried to. It was all meant to be finished by now, if they hadn't overrun at their last job. And if they didn't come now, they wouldn't have been able to fit us in for months."

"Just keep telling yourself that when you get through all this, we've got our holiday to look forward to!" Ollie said encouragingly. "Yep, a few weeks' time and it's 'Hello Ibiza!'"

Kerry felt a rush of excitement. It still hadn't quite sunk in that Ollie was whisking her away on a week's holiday – all on their own – with the money he'd got from his gran for his eighteenth birthday.

"Speaking of which," Ollie rolled his eyes, "is your mum talking to you yet?"

Kerry's frisson of excitement faded away at the mention of her mother who had been less than pleased at Ollie's grand gesture. Well-worn phrases like "you're too young" and "you're getting too serious" were trotted out, even though Graeme Bellamy (and Kerry would be forever grateful to her dad for saying something in her defence) did point out that Kerry was nearly eighteen *and* that she and Ollie had been going out together for a whole year now.

"She's better than she was," Kerry admitted with a sigh. "I guess she realises that with the exams and stress and stuff, she's got to go a bit easier on me. But I'm betting that the minute this stuff's out of the way, she's going to be *right* back on my case."

"Poor babes," said Ollie, cocking his head to one side and gazing sympathetically at her. "Is it really doing your head in?"

Kerry pulled a face and nodded.

"Definitely. It was like, this morning, I couldn't concentrate on anything for the sound of drilling going on in the living room. Then when it stopped for a while, I found myself staring at this page of notes – and I suddenly realised I'd read it about five times and still hadn't taken any of it in!"

"So you thought you'd have a stroll in the fresh air to clear your mind," said Ollie, waving his hands around either side of his head theatrically. "And your feet just happened to turn in the direction of the End, where you knew you could get some tea and sympathy from your understanding boyfriend..."

"Well, I don't know about that," Kerry laughed, "but a Kit-Kat and a hot chocolate might help!"

"Nah," replied Ollie, a sexy grin breaking out on his face and a wicked twinkle glinting in his almond eyes. "C'mere, my little swot-queen and I'll take your mind off all your worries..."

"Ol – no! I mean, there's that customer! You can't – we shouldn't!"

Between whispered protests and giggles, Kerry found herself being dragged off the stool, behind the counter and through the alcove door into the kitchen, empty and silent save for the gentle bubbling of some large covered pots on the cooker.

"Is this private enough for you?" smiled Ollie as he pressed her up against the wall and rubbed her nose with his.

Kerry looked shyly into her boyfriend's soft hazel eyes and nodded, aware of the warmth of his hands around her waist.

"No prying eyes here," he mumbled as his lips touched hers again.

Letting her hands slip around his skinny, taut body, Kerry let all thoughts of exams and grades and parents' expectations and double-glazing fitters slip right out of her mind...

The sudden clatter of footsteps sounded as if it was in stereo.

As soon as Ollie and Kerry broke away from each other, Kerry could see why: Anna Michaels had just barged in the back door of the kitchen, ready to start her shift. Coming through from the front of the café, Nick – fresh from his errands – now stood framed in the kitchen doorway.

Kerry felt her face blush pillar-box red. She knew Nick Stanton would be irked to find his trusted nephew not only slacking on the job, but snogging his girlfriend into the bargain, but she was surprised to see just *how* mad Nick looked. A quick glance over Ollie's shoulder showed that Anna was surprised too; she was hanging back, silently waiting to see if Nick, from his bulging-eyed expression, was about to explode.

"Uh-oh – that's us well and truly nabbed then!" joked Ollie, though Kerry could see from her boyfriend's face that he knew it would take more than a lame joke to wriggle out of this situation.

"That bloke out there," said Nick, nodding back towards the front of the café. "Pay for his meal, did he?"

"Er, no – not yet," muttered Ollie, missing the fact that Nick was speaking in the past tense.

"Well," said Nick, his hands on his hips and his faded Harley Davidson T-shirt stretched tightly across his ample chest, "I don't suppose he will now, since I just saw him hotfooting it out of here when I was coming out of the flat."

"He did a *runner*!" gasped Ollie as the news sank in. "Listen, don't you worry, Nick – I'll go after him and get the money off him right—"

"There's no point," said Nick. "He's long gone – and having a good laugh at my expense!"

"Oh, Nick, I'm sorry! I'll make it up – I'll pay—"

"Hey – listen!" Nick interrupted his nephew, cupping one hand to his ear.

Ollie stopped mid-apology and looked quizzically at his uncle, straining to hear whatever the older man could.

Her heart beating madly, Kerry shot a questioning glance at Anna, who only shrugged her shoulders in response.

"Hear anything, Ollie?" asked Nick, his eyes darting from side to side, his hand still raised to his ear.

"Uh, no," Ollie replied dubiously.

"Neither can I. *That*, Ollie lad," said Nick, lowering his hand and thumping a finger into his nephew's chest, "is because *while* you were through here snogging your little girlfriend, *that* geezer helped himself to my radio!"

Ollie let out a deep groan and knew he'd blown it big time.

CHAPTER 2

FORGIVE AND FORGET...?

"For goodness' sake, Ollie – how old are you? Are you a fourteen-year-old who can't keep his hormones to himself? Don't you and Kerry see enough of each other or something, that you have to sneak through to *my* kitchen to get up to goodness knows what, while *my* business goes down the drain?"

From the relative safety of the front café – still empty of customers – Anna and Kerry exchanged cringing glances as Ollie faced the wrath of his uncle in the kitchen.

Totally mortified by what had just happened, Kerry's first thought when Nick had asked for a moment alone with Ollie was to leg it back home as fast as she could. All of a sudden, studying and noisy workmen were infinitely preferable to hearing her boyfriend get hauled over the coals.

But part of her felt too guilty to leave: she had been kissing Ollie back, after all. And it wasn't as if she'd tried *very* hard to dissuade him from abandoning his waiterly duties...

"While his business goes down the drain?" she whispered to Anna. "It's not *that* bad, is it? I mean, I know it shouldn't have happened, but it's just the price of one breakfast and the radio was pretty old and battered, wasn't it?"

With her finely tuned sense of fair play, Kerry had already worked out in her head the cost of the fry-up that hadn't been paid for. And, as soon as she got home, she was going to look in the Argos catalogue for a similar radio and go and buy it next week, after her first exam was out of the way. But now, from the way he was talking, Nick was scaring her.

"Don't worry – that radio was on its last legs. I think Nick's just exaggerating for dramatic effect," Anna reassured her, pouring tea from the big stainless-steel pot into four mugs. "And you know how fond he is of Ollie – he's probably just a bit disappointed in him and it's coming out worse than he means it to be."

Kerry nodded, her freckled skin pale with strain.

"Look, here's some money – go and put all

Nick's favourite records on to cheer him up," Anna suggested, handing Kerry a bundle of ten pences from the small dish under the counter where they kept odds and ends of spare change. "And I'll see if I can get the guys to come out here and have a civilised cup of tea with us. We might as well take advantage of the fact that we've got zero customers."

Eyes scanning the names of the records in the ancient, wonky Wurlitzer jukebox, Kerry tried to remember which hoary old rock songs Ollie's uncle liked best, but her mind had gone blank. Quickly, hearing footsteps and voices coming out of the kitchen, she hammered in the codes for a Paul Weller track, a Rolling Stones classic and John Lennon's *Imagine* – which seemed a good bet for sending out a message of forgiveness – and hurried over to join Anna, Ollie and his uncle in the booth by the window.

"It's my fault too, Nick," she found herself saying in a tiny voice.

"Aw, forget it, Kerry," Nick shrugged, waving his hand dismissively in the air.

Kerry glanced across at Ollie, whose shoulders seemed to visibly sink with relief at Nick's words. The crisis was over – which was good, considering the temperamental jukebox was up to its usual tricks and had begun to play *Imagine* at twice its normal speed, as if it was being sung by a hyperactive pixie rather than a rock icon.

"Anyhow, anyhow," said Nick wearily, as if the whole confrontation with his nephew had exhausted him, "I've got some news. I was finalising it just now on the phone..."

"What news?" asked Anna, looking slightly concerned.

"Well..." said Nick slowly, dragging the moment of anticipation out, "I'm going to America on Monday."

"*What?*" exclaimed Ollie in surprise. The last thing he'd heard was that Nick was going to take a few days off and maybe visit some old mates in Manchester or just hang out and chill in his flat.

"Yep – I'm going on a 'Home of the Blues' Music Tour. Two weeks, taking in Memphis, Nashville, even Elvis's Graceland..." Nick sighed happily.

"But I thought you saw plenty of America when you used to be a roadie for all those bands years ago?" Ollie quizzed him.

Ollie had grown up hearing all his uncle's tales of endless touring. Plenty of it was true, he had no doubt – it was some of the so-called 'close friendships' with the stars his uncle boasted about that made Ollie have doubts. After all, how many times did wrinkly rockers like Jon Bon Jovi and Tina Turner drop by for a cup of tea in the End?

"Ah, but all you see, being on the road, is the inside of tour buses and the back stages of venues," Nick explained, a faraway look in his eyes as he reminisced. "You never get a feel for where you are. Nope, this time I'm going to see America for real!"

"But, *Monday...?*" blinked Anna, her mind buzzing with the implications for the rest of the staff. "How could you decide that fast?"

"I've had the brochure for months – even got round to phoning and checking the availability a couple of times," shrugged Nick, scratching at the dark stubble on his chin. "It wasn't till the last few days, when I saw how quiet it was here, that I finally thought – go for it, Nick, my son!"

"Good for you!" Ollie grinned enthusiastically. "Wow – wait till Mum and Dad hear about it. They'll be so jealous! I'm pretty jealous of you myself..."

A passion for music was the one thing Ollie's father and Nick had in common. Place the two men side by side and no one would have guessed that overgrown seventies throwback Nick and smart-but-casual pub landlord Stuart were brothers.

"Tell your dad I'll bring him back a stick of rock

from Graceland. Can't say fairer than that, can I!" snorted Nick.

Kerry found herself smiling broadly, not so much at Nick's feeble attempt at a joke, but at the fact that everything was back to normal after a small, uncomfortable blip. Ollie and Nick got on so well – as nephew and uncle, as staff member and boss, as singer and manager – that the last thing they needed was any friction to spoil that.

"It's great that you're going, Nick," Anna butted in, "and I hate to bore you with details, but how are we going to work it with shifts, since you're away for such a long time?"

"Oh, don't worry about that!" said Ollie, before Nick could respond to the question. "We'll get through it. It'll all sort itself out somehow!"

Kerry was suddenly aware of the more serious expression that had slipped back on to Nick's face. Ollie's vague assurances, backed up by precisely nothing, were obviously *not* what the café owner wanted to hear.

"No, Ol – Anna's got a point. It'll need organisation," Nick said earnestly. "Which is why, after what's just happened with that punter, I've decided that while I'm away—"

Both Anna and Ollie hung on his words, waiting to see what plans he was about to come up with.

"—I want Anna to be in charge."

Kerry glanced across the table at both speechless members of staff. Anna was wide-eyed with surprise. Ollie was ashen-faced, apart from a bright pink patch on his cheek, as if he'd been slapped.

Which, to Ollie, was exactly what it felt like.

CHAPTER 3

NO BIG DEAL...

"Ollie! It's for yoo-hoo!" trilled Irene, holding out the phone on the café wall.

"Great!" beamed Ollie, bounding out from behind the counter and heading over to grab the receiver. This empty Saturday afternoon in the End was dragging like mad and talking to Kerry would be a welcome diversion from the boredom that was seeping into his brain. After all, there were only so many times you could clean the tables and hear about Irene's grandchildren's cute little sayings.

"Kez?"

"Wrong!"

"Sonja!"

"Yep. How're you doing?"

"Pretty bored. This place is like a ghost town today."

"How come? Where have all your Saturday shoppers gone?"

"There's engineering works on the line today and the trains have been cancelled. So no hungry people going to and from the city. With that and all the goody-goody swots like you staying home, I've got zilch to do."

"Hey, I'm no goody-goody swot!" Sonja Harvey protested, giggling. "I'll have you know I'm doing a brilliant job of not getting around to looking at my books today. So far I've watched a movie on telly that I shouldn't have, been to see Kerry at the chemist's, given myself a manicure and spoken to Owen for ages on the phone."

"And so what now – you're wasting more time phoning me?"

"Something like that. Actually, I was just phoning 'cause Kerry told me what happened yesterday. Are you OK? Can you talk?"

Ollie yanked over the nearest empty chair and balanced his bum on the back of it.

"Yeah, sure. It's just me and Irene in here at the moment; Nick's nipped next door to Slick Riffs," he explained, keeping one eye on the door just in case there was a sudden rush of customers. "At least that's where he's supposed to be. He's probably out buying a nice pair of Speedos and a sunhat for his holidays."

"Yes, I heard about him going off. So, aren't you gutted?"

"What about?" asked Ollie, wondering what made Sonja think he'd be particularly jealous of his uncle's holiday.

"About him leaving Anna in charge over you!" Sonja spelt out. "Kerry said you were pretty put out about it yesterday."

"Oh, that! No, no, Kerry's worrying for nothing. I was just a bit, y'know, stunned for a minute," Ollie assured her. "Then I realised that Nick didn't mean it – he was just saying that in the heat of the moment, after the mess with that guy doing a runner and nabbing the radio."

"What – did he say that?"

"Not in so many words," shrugged Ollie, rocking back and forth on the chair. "But he's been fine with me today – when he's been here, that is."

"And what about Anna? What did she say about it all?"

"Aw, nothing. It's cool, Sonja – me and Anna'll run the place together like we normally do when he's not around. It won't be a problem."

"Are you sure?" asked Sonja. "'Cause if Nick's really left Anna in charge, it could get weird between the two of you..."

"No way!" laughed Ollie. "We are talking

about Anna here! She's not exactly a power-trip kind of a girl!"

"Well, I don't know, Ol – you know how that old saying goes: 'power corrupts'!"

"Yeah, but whoever came up with that one didn't have hippy little Anna Michaels in mind when they said it, did they?" Ollie joked. "Oh, listen, Son – I've got to go, there's a couple of customers just coming in and I'm going to race Irene to serve them. I'll catch you later, OK?"

Ollie clattered the phone back on to the wall and leapt into action.

What's everyone getting in such a state about? he wondered as he turned the full beam of his grin on the couple who'd just wandered in. *It's going to be no big deal, running this place for the next couple of weeks. I mean, what could possibly go wrong...?*

CHAPTER 4

BEING DISTRACTED

"Joe, sweetie, can you give me a hand with something?"

Susie Gladwin stood in the doorway of her son's bedroom, looking plump, comfy and mumsy, yet simultaneously helpless and little girlish too. The mumsiness was down to her not very fashionable clothes, her verging-on-middle-aged (ie no particular style) hairdo and her general air of smiling friendliness. By contrast, what gave her an occasional look of someone much, much younger were her childlike, soulful round eyes.

And now those eyes were fixed pleadingly on her son.

Joe gazed up from his desk and saw neither his mumsy mum nor her girlish incarnation. All he saw was an interruption to his swotting. It was only five o'clock on Saturday afternoon and he was already well behind with his revision plan.

Taking a deep breath, he resisted the urge to snap at her to wait till later and forced a smile.

"What's up?" he asked, hoping the irritation wasn't obvious in his voice. After all, it wasn't *her* fault he was finding studying such hard graft.

"One of the kitchen cupboard doors is jammed. Can you get it open for me? It'll just take a minute!"

Joe put his pen down and gritted his teeth. He knew that nothing, when it came to his mum and her little requests, *ever* took just a minute.

Half an hour later, Joe had finally found the Phillips screwdriver he needed in the jumble of DIY bits and pieces in the garden shed and was tightening the dodgy hinge on the kitchen cabinet.

"Oh, Joe, that's marvellous – that door's been getting stiffer and stiffer to open lately," his mother gushed, clasping her hands together and looking up adoringly at her son. "What would I do without you?"

Again, her words irritated him – but he knew it was through his own guilt.

Thing is, it's not like I'll be here forever, he thought to himself, the prospect of universities and where his grades might take him looming in his mind.

Not that he wanted to bring it up with his mother at the moment. She'd had enough to cope with lately. She said she'd been fine about Joe's dad getting remarried; hadn't minded that Joe was going to be best man at Robert Gladwin's wedding to the much younger Gillian. She'd even given Joe a card for the happy couple.

But it couldn't have been easy for her, Joe realised, sitting at home alone on that one particular day, knowing that her son was away helping celebrate her former husband's marriage to another woman.

She's amazing really, he thought of his even-keeled, seldom complaining mother.

"Joe – um, since you've got the screwdriver out, you couldn't tighten up the handle of the big frying pan too, could you? It was very wobbly when I was trying to do your fried egg this morning..."

Joe, weighed down by the piles of papers and insurmountable amount of work he knew were waiting for him in his room, felt this was a request too far.

"Mum," he began, about to tell her that he didn't have enough time in the day to tinker with the contents of the kitchen, or any other little odd jobs she had in mind, when the doorbell rang.

"Ooh, I wonder who that could be? Of course, it might be Mrs Andrews from next door," said Susie Gladwin brightly as she scurried out into the hall. "I said you'd give her a hand if she decided to move that old sofa bed out of her spare room for the rubbish collection. You don't mind, do you?"

Joe closed his eyes and wilted. Getting through his mum's sweet-natured shell was going to be harder than he thought.

"Ah, hello! Come on in! Joey will be so pleased to see you!"

Unless it's Jennifer Aniston or someone from the Education Department who's come to tell me personally that exams have been abolished, I doubt that I will be pleased... Joe grumbled silently.

"Hiya!" bellowed Ollie, striding into the kitchen. "What's up with your face? Did you think it was the lovely Meg come to visit, instead of your oldest, bestest friend?"

"No," Joe shook his head at the mention of his new girlfriend's name. "Meg's studying for her A levels – the same as I'm meant to be doing..."

"Yeah, yeah," said Ollie blithely. "I won't stay long."

"Would you like a sandwich, Ollie? I could

make you up a cheese and pickle," smiled Joe's mum hospitably.

"Mmm! It'll spoil my tea... But go on then, if it's not too much trouble!" Ollie said chirpily.

"But, Mum, I really need to get back to work—"

"Oh, now, Joey dear, you *need* to have little breaks when you're studying; it's good for you. Isn't that right, Ollie?" twittered Susie Gladwin, already grabbing a slab of cheddar out of the fridge.

"Too right, Mrs G!" Ollie agreed.

"Now, you boys pop upstairs and I'll bring your sandwiches right up!"

Joe found himself reluctantly treading his way up the stairs, followed by his best friend, who at any other time he'd have been delighted to see.

"What a couple of days I've had, Joe, mate!" said Ollie, flopping back down on the bed and sending a pile of neatly stacked notes flying.

"Why – what's up?" asked Joe, suddenly too genuinely concerned to mind picking up the now jumbled A4 sheets off the floor.

"Well, yesterday, this guy *only* nicked the radio out of the End *and* did a runner without paying when I was on my own in there. And today, incredibly, the place was so dead I thought my head would explode with boredom!"

"Hold up – never mind the stuff about being

bored. What happened with this bloke who stole the radio yesterday?" Joe quizzed his friend.

It shook him up to hear about things like that happening. Especially since it wasn't that long ago that Anna had been caught up in an attempted robbery at the launderette across the road from the café.

"Oh, wow – Nick *totally* flipped out at me for letting it happen. You should have seen him, Joe – his eyes were bulging out like *this*!"

Ollie did a cartoon-style impersonation, then started to laugh at the ridiculousness of it. Joe gave a feeble, confused smile. He didn't know what to think. One minute, Ollie had him all worried; the next he was mucking around.

"Hey – and Nick's *only* going on holiday to America for a couple of weeks," Ollie continued, remembering his other snippet of news. "And get this – he said he's leaving Anna in charge! Can you believe it? What a laugh – as if!"

Joe gazed over at his friend, still lying – propped up on his elbows – on the bed.

"But what made him decide something like that?" asked Joe, bemused.

"Aw, just 'cause he was well miffed about that guy making off with the radio and everything."

"What – Nick's giving you that hard a time for something that wasn't even your fault?" Joe reiterated Ollie's words, full of righteous indignation on his mate's behalf.

"*Wellll...*" muttered Ollie, pushing himself up into a sitting position and looking sheepish. "I s'pose it *was* kind of my fault. Sort of..."

"How do you mean?" frowned Joe. His brain was too cluttered with exam facts and figures to struggle to work out what Ollie was saying.

"Em..." Ollie winced, "...it's just that I wasn't *quite* on my own. Me and Kerry were through in the kitchen and... well, you know how you can get distracted."

Joe could only imagine; Meg – whom he'd met at his dad's wedding – was his first proper girlfriend. Joe and she had kissed, of course, but he hadn't been going out with her for long enough yet to know about being so caught up a girl's embrace that the rest of the world was blotted out.

But Joe certainly knew how it felt to be distracted by a so-called mate who was looking for sympathy for something that was his own fault.

"Joe?" Ollie stared at him questioningly, waiting for him to say something. "What – you think I'm a bit of a dork for doing that, do you?"

"Yep – I guess so," shrugged Joe.

"Well, no need to act like I murdered

someone," said Ollie, his face falling at the sight of Joe's stern expression. "C'mon, what's up with you?"

"Exams," said Joe bluntly. "Remember them? Those annoying things you have to study for?"

"Yeah," replied Ollie, stunned by his best mate's snippy manner. "But what's the big deal? You're smart enough – you'll get by!"

"But that's what I *don't* want to do – I don't want to 'get by'! I want to do pretty well and that's not going to happen if people keep interrupting me all the time!"

Ollie wasn't to know that Joe's head was fit to burst over a whole pile of worries caving in on him. It wasn't just lack of sleep he was suffering from because of exam pressures, or the depressing realisation that the achy feeling he'd had all day meant he was coming down with something just at the wrong time. No, what was *really* weighing heavily on Joe's mind was the news he was keeping from both his mum and from his best friend. The news that only he and Meg knew...

All Ollie *did* know was that it was time to go.

"Sorry to bug you, Joe," he said flatly, getting to his feet and heading out through the bedroom door.

Joe wanted to shout after him, but he couldn't

bring himself to. Sometimes it seemed to him like the whole world revolved around Ollie Stanton, while Joe watched from the sidelines.

He hasn't a clue what's going on with me and he hasn't even bothered to ask, Joe thought bitterly.

Well, now Joe had to make a stand, even if it was just to earn himself the right to get back to his miserable revision.

"I'm not just here at your convenience, Ollie Stanton!" Joe muttered under his breath as his friend's feet pounded down the stairs.

"Don't you want your sandwich, Ollie dear?" he heard his mother's voice drift up from the hall.

• • •

Ollie felt strange – or rather, it felt as if the rest of the world had gone strange on him.

Is it something in the stars? he wondered as he stomped over to The Swan pub where he lived. *I'll have to ask Anna – she knows about all this horoscope stuff...*

To have that unexpected upset with Nick yesterday was one thing; to fall out with Joe now was just too bizarre.

"Hi, honey!" Ollie's mum greeted him as he turned up behind the bar of The Swan to help out. "We weren't expecting you down here till seven. Have you had your tea yet?"

"I didn't want anything – Mrs Gladwin made me a sandwich when I went round to Joe's earlier."

Ollie wasn't one for lying to his parents, but this seemed harmless and it was only a half lie after all. And whether it was Joe's mum's cheese and pickle effort or the thought of the lasagne that needed reheating upstairs in the kitchen, Ollie just wasn't in the mood to face them.

"You're looking a little bit pale – you're not ill, are you?" asked Sharon Stanton with concern, leaning across the bar top to feel her son's forehead.

"No, I'm fine," he assured her, ducking away from her outstretched hand.

"Good – with your Uncle Nick going away, the café would be in a real state if you were under the weather! You just missed him – he was in for a quick pint and a chat with your dad."

Ollie stood stock still and stared at his mum. Did she and his dad know about how he'd messed up the day before? How angry Nick had been with him?

"He's, uh, pretty excited, isn't he?" Ollie ventured, testing the water. It was funny, he'd felt fine about the situation with Nick – had practically forgotten about it, he realised – till Sonja's phone call that afternoon had placed a little niggle of anxiety in his head.

"Excited? He's like a kid let loose in a sweet shop!"

From the way his mother was beaming, Ollie could see that Nick had said nothing about what had passed between them.

That's something, I suppose... he thought to himself with relief.

"Yeah, it's great, isn't it?" he managed to smile, hoping it looked convincing.

"Hi, Ol – hi, Mrs Stanton!" Matt Ryan's voice suddenly interrupted them. "Can I steal Ollie for a minute? I've got something to show him..."

"Course you can! What can I get you to drink?"

"Just a Coke, please – I've got the car. If you can call it that..." Matt laughed.

Matt had only just started to come to terms with having to swap his prized, sporty hatchback for an old rust-bucket. He'd needed the money to pay for some equipment that had been ruined at one of his parties that had got seriously out of hand.

"What've you got to show me then?" said Ollie, glad to see a friendly face. After Joe's unexpected outburst, it was good to see that his other best mate was as normal as usual.

"Look at this!" said Matt excitedly, pulling a rumpled copy of a free paper out of his pocket. "See...?"

Ollie leant over, his eyes scanning the feature Matt was pointing to.

"*Battle of the Bands... open to bands with members aged eighteen and under...*" Ollie read aloud. 'Wow! The prizes are all right, aren't they?"

"Yeah!" enthused Matt. "But read that bit, Ol – *The winning band get an exclusive recording contract*. What about that, eh? Eh? A recording contract!"

Ollie's mind was spinning too fast to reply.

Maybe the stars *were* up to weird and wonderful things at the moment – and this particular ad might be just about the most wonderful thing that could happen to The Loud and to Ollie...

CHAPTER 5

••••••••••••••••••••••••••••

ALL WORK AND NO PLAY

"Maya!"

"What?"

"Phone!"

Sighing, Maya Joshi put down the kettle she'd been about to pour out and padded into the hall.

It wasn't that she couldn't be bothered taking the call – after all, it was bound to be one of her friends and talking to any of them would be a welcome distraction from her swotting this late Monday afternoon. Even fixing a cup of coffee – as she'd just been about to do – was a welcome distraction.

Out in the hall, Sunita leaned back against the wall, idly blowing bubble gum while eyeing her big sister with barely disguised disdain.

"Thank *you*!" said Maya sarkily, grabbing the

phone out of Sunny's uplifted hand and resisting the urge to stick her finger in the pink globe so she could watch it splatter all over her sister's sulky little face.

Not so long ago, Maya thought she might have turned a corner in her relationship with Sunny. After catching her sister smoking, Maya had made a deal not to tell their parents – *if* Sunny stuck to her promise not to mess around with cigarettes again. Some people might have been grateful to have a sister like Maya, who didn't automatically blow the whistle on them and land them up to their armpits in trouble. But not Sunita.

If anything, it seemed to make her resent Maya even more.

"Hello?" said Maya, staring Sunny down until the younger girl finally got the hint to stop hanging around, listening in, and to make herself scarce.

She's probably listening behind the door right now, thought Maya as Sunny disappeared into the kitchen. *Either that or she's gone to spit in my coffee...*

"Hi, it's – *ahhhhhhiiiiyyyyyyaaaaaa* – me!"

Luckily, Maya instantly recognised Cat's voice through her lazy yawn.

"Hi. How's it going, Cat?"

"IT, Maya, is going ALL wrong. And YOU are the only one who can help me!"

Maya smiled to herself. From Cat's tone of voice, she knew that whatever terrible THING had occurred, it wasn't anything that was stressing her friend out too much – not the way Cat was managing to yawn her head off.

"What's up with you? Didn't you get to bed till late?"

"Maya – I was tossing and turning with worry. I didn't get a moment's peace last night!"

"That's not true, is it?" Maya grinned.

"Uh, no," Cat admitted without further ado.

"Well, come on – give me the truthful version of events!"

"OK, OK," said Cat, untroubled at being rumbled so easily. "I'm knackered because I stayed out really late with my mates from college – it was Amanda in my class's birthday."

"And...?" coaxed Maya.

This was entertaining, as anything to do with Cat generally was, but Maya didn't have all year to wait for Catrina Osgood to get to the point.

"Well, one of the girls there – who's a friend of a friend – got totally drunk. She's a complete mess; hasn't been able to get out of bed all day."

Maya rolled her eyes to the ceiling.

"Uh-huh. And tell me, Cat, does this story

have an end? Or should I get a chair and make myself comfy if you plan to ramble on for a while...?"

"Oooh, cheeky!" Cat retorted. "The point is, Anita—"

"—who is...?" Maya interrupted.

"...who is the girl who got drunk – was meant to be my model for today. You know how I'm doing this portfolio of looks? Doing different make-up on different skin types and getting them photographed?"

Maya didn't know – she hadn't seen much of Cat or any of her friends in the last week. But even so, she had a funny feeling she knew what was coming next.

"Let me guess – Anita was your model for Asian skin?"

"Yes! How did you know?" gasped Cat, who was totally unaware how transparent her friends often found her.

"Hey, just my natural intuition," shrugged Maya.

"So listen – is there any chance of you coming along and filling in for her?"

"I can't, Cat. I'm too busy swotting..."

"What? What for?"

"Exams?"

"Yeah, I know. But it's not like you're doing

your A levels, is it? It's only mocks – and they don't count. Come on, you can do it!"

"Cat, I know it's mocks – but they're still exams and I still have to study."

"Oh, I get it. Parents holding you hostage? Not allowed out the front door for two weeks unless it's to be frogmarched to an exam hall?"

Maya flipped her eyes towards the semi-closed kitchen door – she'd have to watch her words, just in case Sunny was earwigging. Being caught complaining about her parents' overzealous attitude towards studying would just be playing into her sister's hands. It would be reported back to them at the first opportunity.

"Something like that," she said, hoping Cat would get her meaning.

"What a drag," Cat sympathised, yawning again. "And what about Alex? Are you banned from seeing him too?"

"Yep," said Maya non-committally.

"And you can't say anything else 'cause your pain of a sister's listening in?"

"Right!" smiled Maya, relieved that Cat had grasped the situation.

"Well, listen – I'd better go and scour the college corridors for another likely face before everyone leaves for the day. Give's a call when you get out of jail!"

"Yes, I will. Hope you find another victim – sorry, model!" Maya teased, before putting down the phone.

Almost instantly, the phone rang again.

A little too quickly – unless she had been standing right behind the door – Sunny burst out of the kitchen.

"*I've* got it," said Maya firmly, her suspicions confirmed. "Hello?"

"Maya? It's me. How's it going?"

It was on the tip her tongue to say Alex's name out loud, but she stopped herself just in time. Of everything in her life, the one aspect that Maya wanted to keep *well* away from the scrutiny of her poisonous sister was her relationship with Alex McKay.

"Hi – I'm OK. A bit snowed under, but OK."

"Good. I won't keep you – I'm going out to meet Gavin soon. We're going to play five-aside."

"What are you going to do the rest of the evening – lie on the sofa and groan?" laughed Maya.

Her boyfriend had only recently started playing football with some fellow lecturers on Monday nights and, from what he'd told her, despite his enthusiasm, he wasn't much cop at it.

"Yes, I probably will!" Alex admitted brightly, laughing too. "Gavin and the others are all going on to some do, but I think I'll stick to a hot bath and a video."

"Why?" asked Maya, suddenly sensing that Alex was choosing the second option for her sake. "Why don't you go along? You haven't been out for ages. Just 'cause I'm stuck in doesn't mean *you* have to do the same."

"I know. I just didn't fancy it. But I s'pose... yeah, it could be a laugh!"

"Of course it could!" Maya encouraged him.

Maya twisted her finger into the coil of the telephone wire as she felt a faint stab of jealousy. Not that she was about to show it; restricting her boyfriend's social life would, in Maya's eyes, seem like a childish impulse. And going out with someone so much older than herself, the last thing she ever wanted to appear to him was childish.

"OK – I will! You're right, Maya – it could be fun. Although it would be *more* fun if you were there too..."

"Well, that's nice of you to say," she smiled coyly. "So what's this do in aid of?"

"It's Melanie's birthday party."

"Oh, say happy birthday from me." Fleetingly, Maya wondered at the coincidence of two phone calls, back to back, both involving birthdays. Cat's classmate she might have met, but couldn't remember. Melanie, who went out with Alex's mate Simon, she'd met loads of times and really liked her.

"So, where's the party going to be then?"

"Just round at her and Holly's flat. I haven't been round there yet since they moved in. Ah – listen, that's a car horn tooting outside. Must be Gav. I'd better go. I'll speak to you later – yeah?"

"Sure," said Maya, hearing the line go dead.

Sure.

Sure, she was reasonable, practical and mature. Sure, she didn't want to put pressure on her boyfriend to give up his social life just because *she* had to for the moment.

But one other thing Maya was sure of was the feeling of unease that had settled over her. She'd met most of Alex's friends and colleagues, even if only briefly in some cases. But the one person she hadn't met yet was Holly – though her name had understandably stuck in Maya's memory banks.

"It was only a couple of dates and then it fizzled out," Alex had explained when Maya had pushed him to list all his exes. But Holly hadn't meant anything to her at the time; just another name on a roll-call of girlfriends that she'd gigglingly forced Alex to tell her about one night. Maya didn't think anything of the fact that Alex had so many names to mention while she had none: she was only seventeen and he was twenty-seven, after all.

But now Holly *wasn't* just a name on a list. She existed in flesh and blood and she would be at the same party tonight as Alex. And Maya wouldn't.

An icy feeling settled over Maya – and she suddenly realised that Sunny was blatantly staring at her from the kitchen doorway.

"Not got anything better to do?" Maya snapped at her sister, before slamming the already-dead phone down and thundering upstairs to her room.

CHAPTER 6

TAKING ORDERS

"*La, la, la, doo-doody-dooooo!*"

Matt and Anna stared at each other and burst into giggles.

"Sounds like someone's happy in their work!" whispered Matt, nodding in the direction of the kitchen, where Irene could be heard trilling along to the radio that Anna had brought down from her flat above the café.

"I hope everyone else will feel the same..." said Anna, giving the counter a quick wipe before setting down two cups and saucers.

Matt's brow furrowed.

"Do you still think Ollie's going to be weird about this?"

"How could he *not* be? I mean, *I* feel weird about it," said Anna frowning. "I'm sure he thought Nick wasn't being serious about it – same as I did. But when Nick came in yesterday, before heading off to the airport, he came out with it again: *I'm* supposed to be in charge. I tell you, I don't feel comfortable about this one little bit."

"Aw, don't worry about it. Ollie seems fine to me," Matt tried to reassure his girlfriend.

"Yes, well, he's not exactly going to say anything negative about me being left in charge to my boyfriend, is he?"

"Your boyfriend, hmmm?" said Matt, smiling mushily at her.

He still hadn't got over the novelty of finally getting together with Anna after a couple of false starts. And he couldn't get enough of her talking about their relationship in such solid terms – in the beginning Anna had seemed so reluctant to let anyone know about the two of them, he'd almost thought she might break it off with him at any minute.

Catching the stupidly adoring look on Matt's handsome face, Anna decided that things weren't so bad after all.

I'm over-reacting, she told herself. *Ollie was just a little bit hurt when Nick said what he did. That's understandable – I'd feel the same.*

"Hey – Nick will be in America now!" Anna

pointed out, pouring tea into the cups and trying to brighten up. "Chilling out, with no worries!"

"Yep. And you should have no worries either," said Matt, returning to Anna's original point. "Ollie's too easy-going to hold grudges. And if he is still hacked off, it's going to be with Nick, not you."

"I know. Anyway, I've decided – whatever Nick said, I think I'll talk to Ollie about running the show together, just like we have any other time Nick's been off. It's always worked that way and what Nick doesn't know won't hurt him."

"Sounds like a good idea," nodded Matt from the other side of the counter.

"Uh-oh – it's the Invasion of the Mini-Brats..." muttered Anna as the door of the End tinkled open and a group of mothers arrived with their small offspring.

"Thought you liked babies!" Matt commented, above the screech and bangs of chair and tables being moved to accommodate buggies.

"Don't mind the babies," hissed Anna, wide-eyed. "At least they stay in one place. This lot are all mobile – they'll be running round here crashing into table legs and trying to hit each other with salt cellars and spoons in a minute..."

"Mmm – think it's time for me to go," said

Matt in alarm. "But give us those teas over first; I'll deliver them to the two old blokes in the corner while you brave the mum posse."

"Thanks!" said Anna, grabbing her pad.

At the same time she took a fleeting look at her watch.

Where's Ollie? she frowned, suddenly realising that he was quarter of an hour late for his shift.

Just at that second, she saw his grinning face at the window as he ran past.

"Hi, Anna!" he said brightly, dodging a Thomas the Tank Engine that was hurtling across the lino.

"Hi!" she waved at him distractedly as the first of the women began to give her order. She felt slightly peeved at his lack of apology for being late.

"Hey, Matt – I got the tape of our songs done for our competition entry!" she heard him say to her boyfriend, who hadn't yet made it out of the door.

"Brilliant!" Matt replied.

"Cappuccino, please. Oh and could you heat this bottle of milk up for me too?"

"One tea and an orange squash. Can she have two straws with that? She likes to have two..."

"And have you got any plain doughnuts – without the icing? He loves the ones with the pink icing but they're *so* bad for his teeth..."

Anna was finding it hard to pay attention to her complicated order. Another tableful of customers had just arrived – four grannies in for a gossip – and in the background Ollie and Matt were still talking.

"I'll need to get this cassette parcelled up and posted," she heard Ollie say, oblivious it seemed to the work at hand. "Listen, Matt – here's the paper. Could you look up the address for me? I'm just going to nip next door to Slick Riffs for a second – there's envelopes and tape in the back office. And I might as well see how Bryan's doing in there, since Nick's left him in the lurch this week too!"

Swivelling round, her order complete, Anna blocked Ollie's exit route between the tables.

"Ollie – those customers have just arrived and I think Irene will be needing a hand to get the lunch menu ready. Can you save your hunt for stationery till your break?"

Anna was irritated, but she was doing her best not to show it, framing her request in a smile.

After Nick making out that he wasn't acting responsibly enough lately, you'd think Ollie would be trying a bit harder – instead of wandering in late and trying to sneak off the minute he arrives! she fumed inwardly.

"Yeah, but I could catch the half-past delivery at the postbox if I do this now. And I want to catch Bryan anyway. Won't be a minute!" Ollie shrugged casually and made to go past her.

"Ollie! I'm *asking* you to leave that till later, *please*!"

She knew the words had tripped out of her mouth too harshly, too bossily, and she could almost feel how frosty her expression was. But Anna was too stunned at Ollie's presumption to stop herself.

"Oh. Uh, right..." said Ollie, his own amiable expression slipping away.

He turned and made his way back to the counter where Matt was perched on a stool, both the paper and his mouth open wide.

"What's up with Anna?" hissed Ollie, tying on his apron and staring in her direction as she took the orders from the grannies.

Matt, caught between loyalty to his girlfriend and his best mate, simply shrugged.

"I'd only have been five minutes!" Ollie grumbled, agitatedly tying his finger into the bow-knot of the apron strings by mistake. "And I just wanted to check Bryan was going to be OK about losing his Monday off. I'm going to be too busy in here to help out like I usually do."

"Nah, it's OK – I'm going to help him."

"What?" blinked Ollie.

"Yeah, Nick phoned me on Sunday, asking me to lend a hand in Slick Riffs," Matt explained, not registering the hurt in Ollie's face. "I'm going in for a couple of hours on Friday and Saturday afternoon to get the hang of things, then I'm in on my own next Monday – when it's quiet – so Bryan doesn't have to change his plans."

Ollie was too stunned to respond. Nick regularly popped through to the second-hand record shop to give Bryan a break, but when proper cover was needed, it was always Ollie who was drafted in. He knew it wasn't practical now, not with the café to run, but the fact that Nick had never even bothered to mention he was going to approach Matt...?

"Oh, no!" gasped Matt suddenly.

"What? What's up?" asked Ollie, noticing that his mate's gaze was fixed on the newspaper and the Battle of the Bands ad.

"*That* can't be right?!" exclaimed Matt. "But this is... oh, no – it's the wrong date!"

"What are you on about?" asked Ollie, cranking his neck round to see what the problem was.

"This is the week before last's copy of the paper – and the closing date for the tapes for the competition is today!"

"You're joking!" gasped Ollie, this latest bad news quickly shaking him out of his reverie.

Anna walked over, noting the boys' shocked expressions.

"What's wrong?" she asked, modulating her voice to sound normal.

She'd felt quite shaken by her little outburst just now; it wasn't really in Anna's nature to get wound up and she was more than willing to start again. And OK, so Ollie still wasn't helping out much yet, but by the look on his face, something was *really* wrong.

"Anna! Total disaster!" said Ollie, his eyes wide and his floppy hair tousled where he'd frantically run his hand through it.

"It's that Battle of the Bands thing The Loud are entering," explained Matt. "The closing date for entries is today!"

"Anna – I'm sorry, but I'm going to have to go up to the city and hand this thing over personally!" Ollie gabbled, untying the apron he'd only just put on. "If I go now I can catch the next train and be back here in under two hours!"

"Ollie! There's no *way* you're going to take off like that and leave me and Irene to it! This is *work* – you can't just swan in and out when you feel like it!"

Ollie's face went as red as Anna's was white.

"That's an order, is it?" said Ollie, his eyes fixed on Anna's.

"Well... Nick *did* leave me in charge," said Anna, a hint of a wobble barely detectable in her voice.

"No problem! No problem!" intervened Matt quickly, leaping off his stool. "I'm not doing anything today – give us the tape, Ol and I'll take a drive up to the city right now. It's kind of my fault anyway, not noticing it was an old newspaper and everything..."

"Thanks, mate," said Ollie flatly as Matt tucked the cassette into his pocket.

"Thanks..." Anna muttered quietly as her boyfriend gave her a hasty peck on the cheek.

For all the chatter and clamour of children going on around them, the silence between Anna and Ollie lay as heavy as storm-laden thunder clouds.

CHAPTER 7

EVERYTHING ALL AT ONCE

"Wow – did it go *that* badly?"

Turning his head to respond to the familiar voice seemed like an enormous effort. Joe's head and back ached, and it wasn't just from the strain of the exam he'd sat through. It felt, Joe knew, more like a case of flu coming on, just as he'd dreaded at the weekend.

"The exam? Oh, just pretty lousy," he shrugged, responding to Sonja's question. "How was yours?"

Sonja smiled brightly and nodded, her straight blonde hair being lifted by the gentle breeze that was playing around their heads.

"It went fine – no questions that caught me out, thank goodness!" she replied.

Joe shivered, pulling his jacket closer around

him. All he wanted to do was get home and switch off. Not that that was an option.

"Joe, don't take this the wrong way, but you look terrible. You're white as a sheet and you've got the darkest circles under your eyes," said Sonja, squinting at him with concern. "Have you been staying up too late swotting or what?"

"No – I think I'm coming down with something."

Sonja took two steps back.

"Don't give it to me then!" she joked. "I've got to do well in my exams to get the grades I need. I don't need your germs clogging up my brains with snot right now!"

"Tell me about it..." Joe muttered, his shoulders hunched against the cold shivers he felt shooting through his body.

"Poor babe, you better go home and get some Night Nurse down you!" Sonja sympathised, from a safe distance. "Or, better still, get Meg to come round and play nurse!"

Joe managed a smile at his friend's cheek. There was nothing he'd like more than to hang out with Meg, with her dark smiling eyes and her cute little cupid-bow lips...

"I *wish*," mumbled Joe. "But it's band rehearsal tonight."

"And it's going to be band rehearsal without a

drummer for once. You can't go if you're feeling that lousy, Joe!"

He knew Sonja was right. But after their small ruction on Saturday afternoon, Joe was keen to get back to normal with Ollie – and rehearsals would provide the perfect opportunity.

If he didn't keel over first.

• • •

"Joe, sweetie, it's not often I put my foot down," said Susie Gladwin, staring at her son with her round eyes, "but I really don't want you going to your band practice tonight. You're not well."

Joe was feeling as soggy as a bowlful of scrambled eggs, but some small reserve of energy still lingered - enough for him to argue back.

"Mum – don't fuss. Rehearsals are only across the road at The Swan. I'll be fine!"

"You might be fine – if you stay in and have an early night! Oh and this came for you," said his mum, passing a letter over while she continued her fussing. "I mean, you've still got another two exams to do and if you go out tonight you'll get all sweaty playing those drums and then come out in the night air... what is it, dear?"

Joe's glazed eyes were fixed on the contents of the letter.

"It's my driving test," he said, not looking up.

"But they've given you a date for it already, in August, haven't they?"

"Yes, but now they've offered me a cancellation. I can sit it a week on Friday, if I want."

Susie Gladwin blinked as she digested this piece of information.

"A week on Friday? But that's your last exam..."

"Yes, but the exam's not till 2.00 pm – the driving test's at nine in the morning," Joe pointed out.

The thought of doing both things on one day made his already wobbly head swim, but it was better than the alternative: wait and worry about the test for the next three months. To get that *and* the dreaded A levels out of the way in one fell swoop seemed the best option he had.

"But that's too much! You can't do both on the same day – that's pushing yourself too hard, love!" his mum protested. "And you're not well! What if you still feel ill next week?"

"OK, OK!" snapped Joe, aware that he was taking his own frustration out on his well-intentioned mother. "I'll pull out of rehearsal, if that's what you want!"

Feeling rotten for blowing up unfairly like that,

and feeling rotten in general, Joe hurried out of the kitchen and headed for the phone.

"Anna? It's Joe – is Ollie there?"

"Sure – just a second."

Anna didn't sound herself, Joe noticed, before instantly doubting himself. After all, he felt so spaced he couldn't trust his own judgement too far.

"Hello? Joe? What's up?"

"Er, hi, Ol. Listen – I'm not feeling too hot... I'm going to have to give rehearsals a miss tonight."

There was an ominous silence before Ollie finally replied.

"Fine. Well, catch you later then."

"Yeah... OK. See you, Ol."

"Yep. Bye."

Joe stared at the receiver. He wasn't sure he'd picked up the right signals about Anna, but he knew he wasn't mistaken when it came to Ollie.

Gee, thanks for your concern – not, thought Joe as he hung up.

• • •

Ollie took a deep breath and walked back over to the table he'd been clearing.

Oblivious to how noisily he was thudding the

dishes on to his tray, Ollie's mind throbbed with this latest piece of bad news. He'd been dying to tell the other lads in The Loud all about the competition and was going to surprise them with it tonight.

Fat chance of that, he thought darkly, now that Joe was the third member of the band – after Andy and Billy – to phone up and cancel in the last half hour. *All because of some stupid exams. I mean, can't they spare two measly hours*?

"Do you have to make that racket?" came Irene's gently teasing voice beside him.

But after a day of feeling that his friends and fate were all ganging up on him, Ollie was – for once – in no mood for jokes.

"Sorry, Irene, but I do," he replied, chucking a handful of cutlery on top of the plates and making the old lady wince at the ear-splitting clatter.

CHAPTER 8

ALL PLAY AND NO WORK

"Who needs A levels anyway?"

"The college you want to get into?" suggested Maya, grinning at Kerry, who was slouched on the red vinyl banquette opposite.

"I s'pose so," smiled Kerry. "Still, after the mess I probably made of that exam, I think I deserve *two* chocolate brownies, instead of one."

"Well," shrugged Maya, "getting wound up by exams takes it out of you. All the worry *must* burn up loads of calories!"

"It must, mustn't it? And you're a doctor's daughter, Maya, so I'll take that as scientific proof! Two chocolate brownies, when you've got a minute, Anna!"

"Uh-huh..." murmured their friend distractedly as she rushed past them, tray in hand.

"*She* doesn't look too happy. Wonder what's up?" said Maya softly.

"Oh, I think it's this whole thing with Nick leaving her in charge over Ollie while he's on holiday," whispered Kerry. "It's made the atmosphere really weird between the two of them."

Both girls surreptitiously glanced over at the long-haired waitress, who was just disappearing into the kitchen.

"Hmm – well, they'd better sort it out," Maya said with a frown fixed on her smooth forehead. "Nick's only been gone three days – they've got a long while to go before he comes back!"

"I know..." groaned Kerry, watching for Anna's return. "Ollie's worried that Anna's being too bossy, like the power's gone to her head, he says."

"But *that* doesn't sound like Anna," Maya pointed out. "Still, she isn't a happy bunny – that's for sure. I wonder if it's something else?"

"Like what?" Kerry blinked. "You mean, like some hassles going on between her and Matt maybe?"

"Maybe... but maybe not. The two of them are pretty happy together. Or at least they *seem* that way..."

Maya looked suddenly flustered and stared down at her hands.

"What is it?" Kerry asked, reaching one hand across the Formica table towards her friend. "Do you know something about Matt and Anna?"

Maya glanced up at Kerry, half shook her head and looked confused.

"Oh, no. I – I think maybe I've got a bit of a downer on love and stuff at the moment."

"How come? Aren't you and Alex getting on?" asked Kerry gently, realising that Maya had been talking more about her own relationship than Matt and Anna's.

"Yes. I mean, we would be fine if we could see each other. But Mum and Dad have put a ban on that – and me going out in the evenings with any of you guys – until these mock exams are over."

"So what's the problem? Think he'll get bored and find someone new?"

Kerry had been joking. Alex was so sweet and sensible – and old enough to know better – and the idea of him running off with another girl just because Maya was out of the picture for a couple of weeks was ridiculous.

But judging by the expression on Maya's face right now, Kerry realised, *that idea isn't as ridiculous as it sounds...*

"Kez, he went to a birthday party on Monday night," Maya began, her dark, almond-shaped eyes wider than usual.

"*And*?" asked Kerry, her heart pitter-pattering with concern. "What happened?"

"And... I don't know – I haven't spoken to him on the phone yet."

Kerry was confused. What was Maya getting at?

"It's just..." her friend winced, agitatedly tearing at a paper napkin. "It's just that I know this will sound stupid, but an ex-girlfriend of his was going to be there..."

"You know something? That *does* sound stupid!" Kerry laughed reassuringly. "Alex isn't going to leap into a snog-fest with some ex just 'cause you're stuck at home!"

Maya wrinkled her nose and gave a little shrug of her shoulders.

"And you know something else?" Kerry continued.

Maya shook her head.

"You said a minute ago that Anna wasn't the bossy type. Well, I'm telling you, *you're* not the jealous type. I think you've just been getting a bit down about stuff because you're tired at the moment, with all your studying. I know *I* am!"

Maya – who normally doled out the good advice in their crowd – nodded gratefully, glad to have someone give her a little perspective on her love-life, and tell her what she already knew. She was overtired, overemotional and just being plain silly.

"Poor Alex. If you go doubting him now, when you're only stressed out by your mocks, what's it going to be like for him when it's your A levels?"

Me and Alex, this time next year?

As the thought ran through Maya's mind, she didn't know what exactly the peculiar tug at her heart was trying to tell her.

• • •

"Amazing..." said Andy, nodding his head as if he could hear some imaginary song playing in there.

"Well, it *will* be amazing if we get shortlisted for the finals!" Ollie pointed out.

"How could they *not* pick us?" beamed Billy, his broad, infectiously enthusiastic grin filling Ollie full of confidence again after last night's no-show at rehearsals.

The two boys, guilty at blowing out their regular Tuesday night get-together, had met up and swung around to the End-of-the-Line café this Wednesday teatime to say their sorrys again and catch up with Ollie. Neither Andy or Billy had expected to hear such exciting news as the Battle of the Bands competition.

Andy seemed so surprised, he plonked himself

down on a stack of bread crates by the back door. Billy, meanwhile, was practically bouncing on the spot in the yard that backed on to the End's kitchen.

"You're right!" grinned Ollie, leaning an elbow back on the iron staircase that led to the upstairs flat. "Why shouldn't The Loud get picked? We're great, aren't we?"

"So when do we hear if we're shortlisted or not?" asked Andy, gazing up at Ollie.

"Don't know. But don't worry, lads," Ollie reassured his guitarist and bass player, "I'm covered every which way. On the application form I gave my number here, at home, at The Swan and even Kerry's – so there's no way I'll miss them if they call!"

"What – you mean you didn't give them the number of the phone box beside the park that you pass on your way to work?!" laughed Billy, forgetting his own exam worries in the excitement of the moment.

Ollie felt jubilant at the other lads' reaction. Now all he wanted to do was to call Joe to tell him the news.

Maybe I was a bit tough on Joe last night, Ollie mused. *He did sound pretty ill. But this news'll cheer him up. I'll give him a buzz after—*

"Ollie – I need a hand inside."

He swung round at Anna's words and saw her framed in the doorway to the kitchen, her face as stern as any schoolteacher's.

"Yeah, in a second, Anna – I'm on my break, remember?" Ollie countered, feeling like a naughty child being reprimanded.

"Ollie, you took your break at five o'clock and it's twenty past now. That's a long ten-minute break by my reckoning, specially when there's a room full of customers out there!"

Infuriatingly, Anna spun away from him before he could answer, but in truth, Ollie couldn't have come up with a very good reply anyway. So it wasn't fair that Anna was angry with him – there had only been two customers in when Ollie had come out to sit and get a bit of fresh air on the back step – but Ollie couldn't really argue about the time. He'd completely lost track of it once Andy and Billy had arrived and they'd got talking.

"Whoooo-OOOOO-ooo! Hark at *her*! Who's been a naughty boy then?!" Billy held up his hands to his chest like a granny clutching a handbag.

"What's up with Anna?" asked Andy more sensitively. "She really snapped at you there..."

"Yeah," said Billy, dropping the jokey stuff and peering into the kitchen after her. "I thought our Anna was a bit of a hippy. Thought she was into peace and love and good karma and that."

"Yeah, but that was before our Anna got on her power trip," said Ollie, feeling hurt and sounding bitter.

"Ollie, I think you'd better give Anna a hand," said Dorothy, peering out into the yard, still clutching the spoon she'd been using to stir the pasta sauce.

"Yep, I'm there, Dorothy," Ollie reassured the old lady, before adding under his breath: "When Sergeant Major Michaels calls..."

Clicking his heels together and saluting at the boys, Ollie turned sharply and marched off into the kitchen.

CHAPTER 9

OLLIE DOES IT AGAIN

"Penny for 'em!"

"Shut up, Matt."

"Come on, love – give's a smile!"

"Matt!"

"Cheer up – it might never 'appen!"

"Matt – quit the bloke-off-a-building-site routine!" said Anna, glaring at her boyfriend as he stood grinning at the open front door of her flat.

But she wasn't really annoyed. He'd done what he'd set out to do: jolly her out of her downbeat mood.

"You *laaaaaaave* it!" he growled, picking Anna up and spinning her round in the tiny hallway.

"Matt! Put me down, you idiot!" Anna giggled, hammering not very hard on his shoulders with her fists.

"That's better – I like hearing you laugh, instead of moaning all the time," said Matt. He stopped spinning and let Anna slip gently down till just the tips of her toes were on the floor.

"'Scuse *me* – I am not moaning all the time! Now, are you going to let me go, so I can get ready for work?" asked Anna, raising her eyebrows at her boyfriend.

"Not until you promise that you're going to cheer up and not moan once today."

"It doesn't quite work like that though, does it?" said Anna, wriggling to get free. "It's not like I've been *looking* to pick a fight with Ollie the last couple of days."

"Yeah, but he's got a lot of stuff on his mind with this music competition. If they get through it could be their big break! And—"

"Matt – I *know* how important the band is to Ollie and I've always been really supportive. I've been to practically all their gigs, haven't I?" said Anna defensively. "But work's work. Much as I'd like to ignore the customers myself sometimes, they *are* there and that's what Nick pays us to do – look after them and not try to skive off like Ollie, to deliver tapes or hang out with band buddies or whatever!"

"Whoah! Don't give me such a hard time – it's Matt, remember, not Ollie!"

Anna – still held in her boyfriend's arms – frowned and again tried to wriggle free. Despite his efforts to cheer her up, she felt Matt was still painting her as the uptight boss lady here, putting a downer on Ollie's fun. Matt wasn't too hot on the work ethic after all – DJing a couple of nights a week was as busy as it ever got for him – and it was probably inevitable that he'd be sympathetic to Ollie and the much more exciting business of the band.

"Matt – I know you're trying to help, but you're annoying me now. I think you should go and let me get ready."

Grabbing both her hands, Matt planted a myriad of little kisses on the backs of them.

"Sorry, sorry, sorry... I'm a git. What can I do about it?"

Matt was pulling such a pathetically cute face that Anna couldn't stop the smile that crept back on to her lips.

"Thinking before you open that big mouth of yours might help," she said, pushing him out through the door and on to the metal stairs that led down to the yard. "Now scoot!"

"I will. But give us a kiss first..."

"Matt! Just go, will—"

Her sentence was cut short as he bundled her in his arms and kissed her hard.

• • •

"I'll get that, Anna!"

Watching Ollie bound over to the wall phone in the End, Anna allowed herself a little smile.

Looks like today is going to be better, she thought to herself, remembering her conversation with Matt earlier that morning. *Ollie's been acting like his normal, friendly self and he's going out of his way to be helpful, like answering the phone there...*

She carried on loading up her tray with dirty dishes and tried not to listen in to Ollie's conversation. But speaking at the level he was, it was practically impossible *not* to tune into every word.

"You're kidding! Wow! Brilliant! And when—uh-huh. Oh... erm, no that should be fine. Yeah, it'll definitely be fine. And I'll get the details in the post from you in the next couple of days? Magic! Can't wait to tell the rest of the lads. Thanks a lot! Bye!"

Anna put her tray down and her hands on her hips.

"Well," she smiled at her friend as he turned away from the phone. "It's congratulations, is it?"

"Yes!" yelped Ollie, punching the air and making the two old men in the corner jump so much that their teacups rattled. "We're in the final six! We're in with a chance of winning a record contract!"

"That's brilliant – well done! So who's the record company? Which label?" said Anna, genuinely pleased for him.

"Uh... I forgot to ask," shrugged Ollie. "Still, who cares – it's a start, isn't it? Radio One, *Top of the Pops*, here we come!"

"Hey, just think – what a surprise for Nick!" smiled Anna, "He'll be so gutted to find out all this has started up while he's been away!"

"Started up? It'll be all wrapped up by the time he's back!" grinned Ollie happily. "We'll already know whether we're on our way to recording our first album or not by then!"

"What – the actual final's happening that soon? When is it exactly?" asked Anna, a nagging worry nipping at the heels of her good mood.

"It's a week on Saturday, up in the city, at some venue called *The Titanic*. Haven't heard of it – have you? Must be new," Ollie mused. "Just time for a few extra rehearsals for The Loud – if I can drag the lads away from their rotten swotting for five minutes of course..."

With that one flippant remark, Anna's good mood disappeared once and for all. Ollie was being totally and utterly selfish, she thought. He'd managed to put down the importance of the other boys' exams and completely ignore his responsibilities to the café, and to her, all in the space of a few short sentences.

"A week on Saturday, Ol?" she queried, giving him a final chance to realise what he was saying.

"Yeah – great, isn't it? 'Course I'll need Saturday off," said Ollie blithely.

Anna clenched her teeth. Once again, he seemed to be ignoring her in all this, making up his own rules as he went along.

"Ollie – you can't take next Saturday off just like that! That's the busiest day of the week and Nick's not back till the Sunday!"

"It's no problem!" Ollie shrugged. "Let's see... it's Dorothy's turn for a Saturday shift then, so I'll just have to charm Irene into covering for me."

"No!" Anna surprised herself by shouting. "You can't just 'charm' Irene – she's away that weekend visiting her family. She's planned it for weeks!"

Ollie stood rooted to the spot, his face as white as the short, starched apron tied around his waist.

"So you're saying I can't go to this competition?"

"I don't want you to miss the competition, Ollie, but there's no way I can give you time off."

"Fine," mumbled Ollie, storming off towards the kitchen. "Boss."

Anna felt eyes boring into her and saw that the two old blokes were listening to every word.

"Better than watching an episode of *EastEnders*, this," said one of them cheerily to her. "What happens next?"

What Anna wanted to happen next wasn't to be: just as she was about to follow Ollie into the kitchen and try to sort things out, the café door tinkled open and several workmen bundled in, in search of hot food and mugs of tea.

How come I'm in the right here, Anna thought, while fumbling for her pen to take their order, *but I'm the one who ends up feeling like Cruella De Vil?*

CHAPTER 10

TAKING SIDES

"Ollie, you look *fabulous*," said Andy, putting on a camp American accent. "But I *really* think you could lose the lipstick!"

"Huh?"

Ollie stood up and looked in the cracked and cloudy mirror on the dressing room wall. Turning his head to one side, he saw the unmistakable imprint of two lips on his cheek - Kerry's kiss marked in soft, shimmery rose-brown.

"Good luck," she'd whispered, just before he and the other lads had left to make their way to the dressing room-cum-storeroom before they took to the stage for their regular Thursday night slot at the Railway Tavern. "Hope the boys aren't too disappointed..."

Of course they're going to be disappointed,

thought Ollie, rubbing the lipstick smear away with his sleeve. *I mean, what do I say to them? Hey guys – we got into the finals! Hurrah! And guess what – we can't go! Boo!*

Turning away from his frowning reflection in the mirror, Ollie got ready to blurt out what had happened.

"Um, before we go on, lads..." he muttered, grabbing the attention of Andy, Billy – who was tuning his guitar – and Joe, who was snuffling into his hankie.

"What's up?" asked Billy.

"Got one of those good news, bad news situations," Ollie shrugged with an apologetic smile.

"Go on then," encouraged Andy.

"Um – I'll start with the bad news. I'm working in the End a week on Saturday and, with Nick away, I can't get out of it."

"Huh?" grunted Billy, totally confused.

"Well, the *good* news is – *would* have been – that we got through to the Battle of the Bands final," Ollie continued, hoping his jokey, roundabout explanation might somehow soften the blow.

"And the finals – let me guess – are a week on Saturday?" said Joe through his blocked nose.

"Correct," nodded Ollie.

"But couldn't you wangle it somehow? Swap a

shift or something?" asked a crestfallen Andy.

"Nope. I've been told in no uncertain terms by Anna that that's a no-go."

"But that's not fair!" Billy moaned. "You lot are always doing each other favours and swapping shifts in that place!"

"Tell me about it..." sighed Ollie. "Andy, Billy – you both saw how Anna was with me yesterday at the caff. At the moment, what she says goes and there's no point arguing with her. God knows I've tried."

"Yeah, but you can't really blame Anna."

Ollie, Andy and Billy turned round as one and gazed in surprise at Joe, who was sitting hunched on a plastic chair, his eyes and nose a matching shade of chapped red.

"C'mon, Joe! Whose side are you on?" asked Ollie, looking at his best friend with righteous indignation.

"I'm not on *anyone's* side," Joe argued wearily, too fluey to get worked up. "But if Nick's not back then Anna couldn't exactly cope with a busy Saturday on her own, with only the two old dears helping out."

"Irene's off too," said Ollie shortly. "But, gee – I'm really glad to have your support, Joe," he went on, a hint of sarcasm creeping into his voice. "It's funny, y'know, you didn't seem that interested when I told you about the competition yesterday and you don't seem that upset about not being able to do it now. It's obvious you're not too bothered at all about the future of this band."

Joe winced.

The future of the band was something he'd been thinking about a lot lately, but not in connection with the competition finals and being able to do them or not. It was to do with his secret – his and Meg's.

And Ollie wasn't being fair. The only reason Joe hadn't been very enthusiastic when Ollie had phoned the previous day was that he'd literally just woken up after dozing off over his books. With a head woozy with germs and sleep it had been hard to take in what Ollie had been telling him.

"Lads – time you were on!"

Derek, who ran the Railway Tavern, had popped his head round the dressing room door and was smiling cheerily at the boys. But his smile quickly wavered when he sussed that he'd interrupted something serious.

"Better get out there..." Ollie muttered flatly to the other lads, although playing together on a small stage was just about the last thing any of them – especially a hurt Ollie and a sickly Joe – were in the mood to do.

• • •

The pub itself was packed this Thursday night, but The Loud's regular band of supporters were thin on the ground.

There was no Maya – courtesy of studying – and therefore no Alex. Cat had defected to a college night out and Anna hadn't shown up yet.

Matt, as ever, was manning the mixing desk. Idly waiting for the boys to take to the stage, he waved over at the small table where Sonja and Kerry were sitting.

"Excuse me, is anyone using this stool?"

"Yes, sorry – we're expecting a friend!" Sonja explained to the woman hovering by them.

"No – it's all right, you can take it," Kerry contradicted her best mate.

"What are you doing? asked Sonja, her two blonde arcs of eyebrow practically touching as she frowned. "Anna'll probably still make it – she'll just be running late!"

"I don't think so. I don't think she's planning on coming..."

"But why? Why not?"

"Oh, Son – it's all got much worse between Anna and Ollie!" Kerry gushed, glad at last of a chance to tell Sonja what had been happening since the weekend. With exams getting in the way, there had just been no opportunity to catch up with her.

"Worse? How?"

"You haven't heard yet, but there's this big competition happening next weekend – the Battle of the Bands – and The Loud got through to the finals. The prize is amazing: the winner gets a record contract—"

"Wow!" Sonja interrupted. "The lads must be so excited!"

"Not *exactly*. Ollie's explaining to them right now that they're going to have to pull out."

Kerry's eyes twinkled as she talked – partly because the room's low lights were glinting in her contact lenses, but also partly because of the threatening prickle of tears that was forming. It wasn't that she couldn't understand Anna's predicament, it was just that Kerry had never seen Ollie look and sound quite so dejected and down before. "It was like our big break, Kez, and now it's just going to slip right past us!" he'd whimpered to her earlier as she tried – and failed – to comfort him.

"Pull out of the competition? Why would they have to do that?"

"It's a week on Saturday – and Anna won't let Ollie have the day off."

"You are joking!" gasped Sonja. "What's she playing at?"

"She says that with Nick still being on holiday—"

"But what kind of excuse is that?" asked Sonja, holding her hands palm upwards in exasperation. "Surely when it's this big a deal, Anna could cope for one stupid day! I *said* to Ollie that it could all get weird once someone gets a taste for power!"

"But then again, I suppose from *Anna's* point of view—"

"Oh, hold on, Kez – Matt's trying to attract our attention. What does *he* want?" Sonja frowned over at her friend, who was unaware that he was interrupting an important conversation. "Look, I'd better nip over and see what's up. Then I want you to tell me every little detail about what's been going on!"

Sonja stood up and wriggled her way quickly through the throng of customers till she reached the mixing desk.

"Hey, Son – I've been waving at you for ages. Didn't you see me?"

"Me and Kez were talking," shrugged Sonja, suddenly feeling irritated by her friend. She knew it was unfair – it was really Anna she was annoyed with right this second, but Matt seemed close enough in the heat of the moment. "So what do you want?"

"Listen, do us a favour. Could you take this

and keep it over beside you?" asked Matt, handing her his padded black jacket. "It's pretty mobbed in here tonight and I don't want someone nicking my mobile out of it while my back's turned."

"Sure," said Sonja, studying Matt's face for clues as to what he was making of the situation between his girlfriend and his mates in the band. But Matt's expression seemed contentedly blank.

"The band's kind of late coming on tonight, aren't they?" Matt commented, glancing down at his watch and back up at the as yet empty stage, unaware of Sonja's scrutiny. "It's nearly ten past. They're obviously missing Nick – he'd have chased them out of the dressing room by now."

"It's a wonder they want to play at all tonight, after the news they've just had," said Sonja drily.

"What news?" asked Matt, turning to face her.

"Just the small, insignificant fact that Anna's ruined their chances of getting a record deal!"

"Whoah! What are you on about, Son?"

"What – haven't you heard yet? Didn't Ollie tell you what Anna's done to him?"

"I haven't spoken to Anna today... and I got down here late tonight..." Matt blinked his explanation, his mind racing. "What are you talking about? What's going on?"

Matt had ended up helping Bryan out in Slick Riffs that afternoon and had meant to pop in to see Anna when the second-hand record shop closed for the night. But Bryan – knowing that Matt was a bit of music gear buff – had invited him back to his flat to check out his new sound system. Matt had spent a happy couple of hours talking 3D bass and super-woofers with Bryan, and had arrived at the Railway Tavern with just enough time to set up his mixing desk and no time at all to catch up with Ollie or any of the others.

"What's going on? Well, Matt – maybe you'd better ask Anna yourself," said Sonja airily. "Obviously, guilt's the reason she hasn't turned up tonight..."

A movement on stage caught the attention of both of them and Matt fumbled quickly with his levels as Ollie said his hellos into the mike.

Flicking his eyes round for a second, Matt saw that Sonja had left his side and was making her way back to join Kerry. He felt totally flustered and confused by what his friend had just said – and by her attitude towards him.

So Anna and Ollie haven't been getting on too great this week, he thought quickly as he watched the lads in The Loud pick up their instruments and get ready to start their first number. *But something's happened today and by the sound of it, it's big...*

• • •

"*And she's out there, out there, waiting for—*" SSScccrreeeeeeeeeeech!!

The couple who'd just walked in the door at the start of The Loud's set gasped. In fact, the terrible howl of feedback squealing over the vocals made the whole audience in the Railway Tavern grimace at once.

"Yikes!" said the girl, clapping her hands over her ears, her short, cropped, spiky red hair standing to attention. "I thought you said this lot were good!"

"They are!" the tall, skinny guy assured her. "It sounds like there's trouble over at the mixing desk. Wonder what's going on with Matt?"

The girl tentatively took her hands away from her ears and gazed at the four lads on the stage, all carrying on manfully, despite the electronic glitch that had interrupted their song.

"Mmmm – who's the singer?" asked the girl, her eyes suddenly glued to Ollie as he began to belt out the chorus.

"That's Ollie," the tall bloke replied in a friendly Glaswegian growl. "Fancy him then, do you?"

"You know me – I always make a beeline for the cute ones," laughed the girl, resting her head on his shoulder and gazing up at him. "Well, I fell for you, didn't I, Alex McKay?"

Alex smiled down nervously at her and twitched his arm just enough to make her move her head away.

"Steady – Maya's friends are here, remember? I don't want anyone getting the wrong idea..."

"Don't worry," she grinned at him. "I'll be discreet!"

The girl reached across and wrapped her fingers around his, giving them a conspiratorial squeeze.

CHAPTER 11

A PRICKLY SUBJECT

Sitting alone on a bench in the schoolyard, Maya squeezed her eyes tightly shut and ran through a brace of equations again in her mind.

"Dreaming of anything nice?"

Opening her eyes, Maya was greeted by Sonja's beaming smile.

"I wasn't dreaming and it wasn't nice, unfortunately," smiled Maya. "And what are you looking so happy about? Don't you have an exam today too?"

"I certainly do, but what's the point in freaking out about it? Either I know my stuff by now or I don't," shrugged Sonja matter-of-factly.

"And knowing you, you do," Maya commented.

Sonja was that rarity: someone who found

exams relatively stress-free, while practically everyone else around her was quietly cultivating ulcers. Of course, she had another incentive to swot up properly for her exams – getting the right grades would guarantee her a place at the university closest to her boyfriend Owen. And making that happen was Sonja's number one priority.

Maya glanced up at the clocktower that dominated St Mark's School and saw that she still had a bit of time before she'd have to make her way to the exam hall.

"So how was the gig last night?" she asked. "What did I miss?"

"Oh, only *everything*," said Sonja, her pale blue eyes wide. "There's big ructions happening between Anna and Ollie. Anna's being such a bitch to him – she's wrecking his career! I can't believe she's got so power-crazy! I'd ask Owen about it but I think he'd get all defensive. He's always so protective of his little sister, just like Peter is with me. I just don't know whether to bring it up with him or not. What do you think?"

"*What?*" Maya responded with shock. It wasn't Sonja's question that bothered her. It was the fact that things had obviously deteriorated since she and Kerry had spoken about it in the End a couple of days previously.

"Can't tell you now – it would take too long," said Sonja tantalisingly. "How are you fixed later? We could meet up for a coffee this afternoon and I'll fill you in."

"Uh, right. Where – at the End?"

"I don't think so!" laughed Sonja. "Not since I'll be talking about the two people who work there! What about the coffee stand in the park, about 4.30 pm?"

"Yes, sure," said Maya, feeling bewildered and upset by this mysterious piece of news. She didn't know how she could concentrate on her exam with all that hanging over her head.

"Listen, I've got to run. Catch you later, yeah?"

Maya nodded at her friend, who had turned to make her way towards the sixth-form college annexe.

"Oh, Maya – I totally forgot!" Sonja suddenly called back to her. "Um, Alex turned up at the gig last night..."

"Did he?" Maya replied, a smile instantly coming to her lips at the mention of her boyfriend. "What did he have to say?"

"Not a lot," said Sonja, looking uncomfortable. "He was with someone. A girl with cropped red hair. Can't remember what he said her name was. Molly or something?"

Maya stared at her friend without actually

seeing her. She'd spoken to Alex earlier the previous evening – their teatime telephone catch-ups becoming a ritual during their enforced separation – and he hadn't mentioned that he planned to go and see the band that night. Not that she minded; Maya spent a lot of time worrying that Alex felt too old to have anything much in common with her crowd of mates. The fact that he wanted to see the band even though she herself wasn't going would normally have been a good sign.

But not in this instance.

"Maya – sorry, I really have to go," Sonja called over. "Look, we'll talk about this later too, OK?"

Feeling numb, Maya gave another half-hearted nod in response.

Alex had been pretty vague about events when he'd told Maya about the house party he'd been to on Monday night. There'd been no mention of talking to anyone in particular, and no mention of Holly – but from what she remembered about Alex's one-time description of her, she was a hundred per cent sure that the girl with the cropped red hair was Holly.

So what the hell's he doing, thought Maya, an icy shiver shooting up her back, *taking his ex-girlfriend out while I'm stuck at home, none the wiser?*

CHAPTER 12

ANNA BLOWS A FUSE

"Hey, you!"

"Hey, you! What are you doing here at eleven o'clock on a Friday morning?" Ollie grinned at his girlfriend as she slid into the empty window booth.

Kerry hauled a heavily packed bag up on to the table, started undoing the buckles and pulled out a couple of note-stuffed ring-binders.

"What brings me here is two noisy double-glazing fitters who're hammering the house apart and singing along at the tops of their voices to a scratchy tape of Oasis – while I'm trying to swot."

"Could be worse; they could be playing Bryan Adams," Ollie laughed, reaching over and giving the table a quick wipe. "Anyway, how can you slag off Oasis? That's sacrilege, that is!"

"Ol, you know I like Oasis. But when you've heard every track forty times and you can't hear Liam Gallagher's voice 'cause a big Geordie called Bruce is howling out the words to *Dont Look Back in Anger*, it tends to lose its charm."

"Point taken. But I thought they'd finished at your place at the beginning of the week?"

"They've come back just for today, to finish off, whatever that means."

'Probably means they're going to charge your mum and dad for extra work that they could have done when they were there before. Oh, well, if you want peace and quiet to study, you've come to the right place. Ever since the breakfast time rush, it's been dead as a very dead dodo in here – Irene and me have had more breaks than we know what to do with," said Ollie, straightening up and tossing the damp dishcloth over his shoulder. "That is, it'll be quiet until the regular Friday mum-and-baby tribe arrive – then it'll be so noisy you'll be glad to get back to Bruce and his yodelling!"

"I'll take my chances," Kerry smiled. "So is it just you and Irene at the moment? Anna doing a late start, is she?"

Ollie glanced quickly in the direction of the kitchen, then crouched down conspiratorially beside his girlfriend.

"She's due in any minute," he whispered, even though the banter of the Radio One DJ was loud enough to drown him out. "Listen, I've got some good news, Kez."

"At last! I thought you looked in a pretty good mood this morning!"

Kerry hadn't even heard what he was going to say, but a wave of relief washed over her. He must have made it up with Anna – that was the only thing it could be.

Or maybe he's cleared the air with Joe, she suddenly thought. *That would be just as brilliant to hear...*

With all the tension going around at the moment, Kerry was starting to feel more and more down as the week progressed. First it was Anna and Ollie rubbing each other up the wrong way, then it was Ollie and Joe, and last night it had got even worse; Sonja had got on her high horse about the whole competition thing and snapped – unfairly, Kerry knew – at Matt. And if *that* wasn't enough, she and Sonja had spotted Alex at the Railway Tavern bar at the end of the night, looking very pally with some pretty redhead who most definitely *wasn't* Maya.

Kerry had gone to bed with a headache as a result and had woken up with an even worse one, fuelled by the noisy double-glazing racket going on at home. The headache was then accompanied by a nervous tummy flutter as she'd made her way along to the End, dreading how things might be with Anna. Would she be curt with Kerry, as an offshoot of what was going on between her and Ollie?

But now Ollie had good news and Kerry couldn't wait to hear what it could be.

"Kez – it looks like..." Ollie couldn't resist teasing her by building up the suspense.

"Like what? Get on with it!"

"Like we *will* be able to do the Battle of the Bands thing after all!"

"Ollie that's brilliant! But how?!" gasped Kerry, wondering what had made Anna change her mind.

"Well," said Ollie, winking at her, "let's just say I haven't lost my boyish charm..."

• • •

Anna frowned at the sight of the white splodge on a spiny leaf of the palm tree that Matt had given her and which now stood sentinel outside her front door.

"Gee, thanks," she muttered to the long-gone bird that had left its calling card on her plant.

Then she shook herself, realising how silly it

was to get annoyed by a spot of bird poo after the relaxing start she'd had to her morning. Trying to tune out the just audible clattering going on in the café downstairs, Anna had put on a laid-back CD and run herself a deep bath that smelled deliciously of magnolia and calendula aromatherapy oils.

Luxuriating in the warm water, she'd given herself a little talking to. OK, so it wasn't her fault that things had gone awry with Ollie, but it would be to her own advantage, as well as Ollie's, to try and make amends.

She couldn't change her mind about Ollie getting the day off for the band competition the following Saturday – there was no one else who could fill in at the café, considering the only other person who often lent a hand was Ollie's fellow band member, Joe – but she could talk to Ollie about it today and explain how truly sorry she was that it had to be that way.

He's too sweet and funny to fall out with, she smiled to herself, turning away from her plant and clattering down the metal steps that led to the backyard below. *So, he's been a bit self-absorbed and thoughtless recently – but people can't be perfect all the time. He's bound to be different today, now that he's had time to let it sink in and realise there was nothing I could do about—*

Anna pushed open the back door of the kitchen and stopped in her tracks.

"Irene!" she yelped, running across and grabbing the grey-haired woman away from the open oven door. "What are you doing? You were just about to pull that baking tray out without any oven gloves on! You could have burnt your hands!"

"Oh! I – I – oh, silly me! I just— I just wasn't thinking!" Irene was flustered, blinking in surprise at her close call.

"Sit down a minute," said Anna, ushering the older woman over to a wooden stool. "That's not like you, Irene; you're always so careful. Are you feeling all right?"

"Ooh, my mind was just in a bit of a tizz, that's all," said Irene, flapping her hands as if to banish Anna's concerns.

"What about?" asked Anna, unused to seeing down-to-earth and cheery Irene looking so frazzled.

Irene scanned Anna's face as if she were trying to make up her mind what to say. Then she rolled her eyes and sighed.

"You mustn't be annoyed with him..."

Anna hesitated. She could practically hear the alarm bells jangling in her mind.

"Who – Ollie?"

"Yes... but promise me you won't be annoyed. I mean, I know you already told him I couldn't work next Saturday, but you can't blame the poor lad for asking again. And I'm sure my brother won't mind if I change the date of my visit to another weekend..."

"Ollie asked you to do his shift?!" asked Anna incredulously.

Without another word, she strode out of the kitchen through to the front café, where she could see Ollie sitting talking to Kerry in the window booth. Luckily, there were no customers in – although Anna was so cross she wasn't sure she'd have been able to have a civilised word with her co-worker anyway, even if the place had been packed.

"Ollie!" she barked.

He spun round, the smile on his face fading in the glare of her scowl.

"How *dare* you bully Irene into agreeing to swap shifts with you!"

"But I didn't bully her! I only asked—"

"You as *good* as bullied her! She's in there now in a real state – it's her brother's Golden Wedding party next week and, thanks to you, she nearly burnt her hands while she was worrying how to break it to him that she couldn't come!"

"But I didn't know that! I didn't think—"

"No – you *didn't* think and that's the problem. You haven't been doing much thinking at all lately," said Anna, hands on hips, and uncharacteristically angry words spilling from her mouth. "The only thing you *have* been thinking about is yourself – what *you* want to do, what *you* want to happen. Well, here's a shocker, Ollie Stanton – the whole world doesn't revolve around you. And I'm very sorry about the competition, but Irene *isn't* going to give up her weekend for you, so you better just get used to the idea!"

With that, she turned and stormed back to the kitchen.

Ollie and Kerry stared at each other over the table, too stunned by the barrage to speak.

"*...so it's stormy, stormy, stormy today, I'm afraid!*" the voice of the newsreader boomed from the radio, his weather forecast predicting more than he could possibly have realised.

CHAPTER 13

CAT TO THE RESCUE?

Passing the newsagent's window, Cat's attention was grabbed by what she saw.

Hesitating, she turned to the window and gazed up and down at the dazzling vision in front of her.

"Not bad. Not bad at all, girl!" she smirked at her reflection, twisting this way and that to strike the best pose in her cute cropped trousers and chunky Buffalo trainers. The orange padded sleeveless vest was another new purchase and she'd accessorised it by tying her blonde hair into two bunches using vivid tangerine scrunchies.

Her eyes flickered slightly to the right, where the newsagent stood, mouth agape, watching her, a postcard he was just about to put in the window still clutched in his hand. Leaning forward, Cat cheekily blew him a kiss and skipped away giggling.

"Yoo-hoo!"

Just as she was about to cross the road over to the End-of-the-line café, Cat heard an unmistakable sing-song voice.

"Hi, Vera!" she chirped, swivelling round to see the mad old lady who ran the launderette waving to her.

"C'mere a minute, dear," said Vera, waving her inside.

Cat smiled to herself as she trotted into the suds-smelling shop. It was Saturday morning and she was in no rush to do anything in particular, so wasting a few moments seeing what Vera had to say for herself could be fun.

"Ooh, let me turn that down for a second," tsked Vera, fiddling with the volume control on her radio. "Can't stand that housey music, can you? Now Boyzone – they're a lovely bunch. Nice lads and such nice tunes, don't you think?"

Cat shrugged and tried not to laugh. From the window of the End, Vera, on the other side of the road, was an entertaining sight, constantly spinning and singing her way around the washing machines and puzzled punters, with only her mop for a partner. But obviously 'housey' music didn't get her toes tapping.

"What's up, Vera?" asked Cat, trying not to stare at the blocks of blue eyeshadow that Vera had smeared unsubtly over her eyelids.

"Well, I'm a bit worried about your friend Anna."

In Vera's eyes, Anna could do no wrong after she'd been her guardian angel and come running to the old lady's aid when thieves tried to rob the launderette a few weeks before. Now it seemed that Vera was trying to repay the favour by looking out for Anna this time round.

"Why are you worried, Vera?" asked Cat, peering over in the direction of the café. She'd been involved in a lot of college stuff lately and hadn't spoken to any of the crowd apart from Maya earlier in the week. Suddenly, she wondered what she'd missed.

"I don't know what's going on, my love, but I do know that Anna's been very down the last few days. I've been watching – and she looks miserable as sin, not her usual, lovely self at all," said Vera, shaking her head and tutting. "I did catch her yesterday when she popped over to Mr Patel's for a magazine, but she wouldn't tell me what was wrong – she just shook her head and said she was fine. But she's not fine – and I think it's got something to do with the lovely lad in there. You know, what's-his-name that looks like a sheepdog."

"A sheepdog?" Cat repeated, wondering who or what Vera was on about.

"Yes, you know – your friend! The good-looking lad who always has his hair in his eyes!"

"Oh, you mean Ollie!" giggled Cat, catching Vera's drift and laughing at the idea of her mate with his floppy fringe being likened to a large, hairy pooch. Only Vera could come up with that one.

"Yes, yes – Ollie! That's it! Anyway, I'm *sure* they're not talking. And I'm *sure* they had a row yesterday morning. I could see them. That other girl was there... your friend... Curly-Wurly..."

Cat furrowed her eyebrows at the mention of a chocolate bar. Then it clicked.

"Kerry? With the curly, reddy-brown hair?"

"That's the one!" Vera clapped her hands.

"I wonder what Anna and Ollie could be fighting about..." Cat mused.

"Well, that's what I called you in for. They're both such sweet young people, but Anna's not going to tell a silly old lady like me all her problems. But maybe she'll tell you. Maybe she needs a friend..."

"Sure. I was on my way over there anyway. Thanks for letting me know, Vera!"

"That's all right, dear!" Vera called after Cat as she left the launderette.

Bouncing across the road in her double-decker Buffalos, Cat's mind was racing. Vera wasn't the only one who thought of Anna as a bit of a saviour – she'd helped Cat out of a bad patch not so long ago, giving her lots of advice and support in the aftermath of an assault Cat had been through.

Anna's always the one doling out advice, thought Cat, speeding towards the café. *But if she's in need of some help, I'm here to give it...*

• • •

"Poor Ollie," muttered Cat as Anna came back over to the counter with an empty tray in her hand.

"*Thanks*, Cat!" said the flustered-looking waitress, checking her order pad and pulling down two clean cups from the shelf.

"No – I didn't mean it like that, Anna! I just meant I can see how disappointed he must be. He must feel like he's letting the other lads down too," Cat tried to explain herself.

Vera had been right – it did seem as if Anna had been looking for a friend to listen. Taking advantage of Ollie being away for an early lunchbreak, it hadn't taken Cat long to push Anna to tell all, even if it was a disjointed story, with

Anna dashing back and forth to serve customers all the while.

Anna suddenly stopped what she was doing and sighed. "That's the problem – I *can* see it from Ollie's point of view too and it makes me feel awful. But what can I do? And what hurts most of all is that Ollie can't seem to see it from *my* side at all..."

A ping from the back kitchen alerted Anna to the fact that a customer's baked potato was ready and she vanished for a second to collect it from Dorothy, who was beavering away with the lunchtime cooking.

Cat swivelled on her stool and drummed her perfectly painted nails on the countertop. Something was going to have to be done to sort things out between her two friends. But what?

If Maya wasn't chained up at home, she'd *sort them out*, thought Cat, who was always in awe of Maya's negotiating skills.

Anna reappeared through the kitchen doorway carrying a steaming baked potato and beans at the exact same moment as a solution zapped into Cat's mind.

"Got it!" squealed Cat, practically jumping off her stool.

"Er, that's nice," said Anna dubiously as she moved round the counter. "I'll just drop this off then you can tell me what it is you've got."

"No, hold on!" said Cat excitedly, grabbing at Anna's arm so that the beans slid menacingly towards the edge of the plate. "Listen – this'll work! Ollie gets to go to his competition; you two make up—"

"Cat!" Anna exclaimed, straightening the plate and glancing over in the direction of the customer to check he hadn't noticed how close his lunch had come to slopping on the lino. "What are you on about?"

"Me, Anna! I'm your way out!" Cat grinned. "I'm your new waitress! Well, for next Saturday, anyway!"

It wasn't Cat's fault this time – at least not directly.

Anna was struggling so hard not to laugh out loud that she didn't even realise that her hand was shaking, sending baked beans splattering to the floor.

CHAPTER 14

MAKING THINGS WORSE

"Do I get the feeling you're not getting up off of there for the rest of the night?"

Anna had just about enough energy left after a hectic Saturday shift to raise her eyes towards her boyfriend. She felt as if her whole exhausted body was melting into the sofa.

"I'll take that as a yes," said Matt, plonking a cup of Anna's favourite herbal tea down on the coffee table. "Is there something I can do to make you feel better? Tell you a couple of my best jokes maybe? OK, here goes. What's brown and sticky?"

"A stick. You've told me all your jokes, Matt," Anna mumbled wearily.

"Right. No jokes. What if I massage your back? Will that make you feel better?"

Matt was surprised at Anna's sudden blast of giggles.

"A massage?" laughed Anna. "You're rubbish at that sort of thing. It's like being prodded in the shoulder blades with a bunch of frozen carrots."

"I'm not *that* bad!" Matt protested, flopping down on the floor beside the sofa.

Anna was great at massages; she had a book on shiatsu massage and Matt was a more than willing guinea pig for her to practise on. She'd tried a couple of times to show him how to have a go himself on her own back and neck, but it felt more like being held in a Vulcan death grip than anything remotely relaxing.

"Sorry, Matt, I don't mean to be ungrateful. Thanks for the thought," said Anna, reaching across and stroking his cheek. "But what's going on today? What is it with people offering to do things that they're completely rubbish at?"

"You mean like Cat offering to help you in the café next Saturday?"

"Uh-huh," muttered Anna, leaning over for her herbal tea.

"But I don't get it – why is it such a terrible idea?"

"Matt, think about it. For one thing, she'd start whimpering the minute she chipped a nail and, more important, have you known Cat to have a job *ever*?"

Matt shook his head.

"But that doesn't mean you shouldn't give her a try, Anna. After all, Nick's giving me a go in the record shop and I've never done that kind of thing before."

"But that's totally different! For a start, you know about music; I wouldn't trust Cat round a kitchen in a million years. And the record shop only gets about three customers a month. I couldn't have Cat mucking things up on our busiest day of the week!"

"Still, I'm sure she'd be on her best behaviour and try really hard..."

"You're being very persuasive, Matt," said Anna with a knowing smile. "Is this 'cause you want Ollie to get the time off? Still on his side more than mine?"

He knew she was only teasing him, but Matt didn't know how to respond. Yes, he wanted the band to go forward into the finals – after all, the whole competition thing had been his idea – but right now, he wasn't sure how he felt about Ollie. Sonja's vindictive outburst on Thursday night had sent him reeling. Was all that down to Ollie bitching to her about Anna? Matt couldn't be sure.

"Course I'm on your side! We go out together. That's part of the rules, isn't it?" Matt blustered.

"Well, you must be about the only person,"

said Anna wistfully, blowing at the hot liquid in her cup to cool it down. "I've hardly seen any of the others in the café in the last few days... It's like they're showing their support for Ollie by staying away."

"Nah, that's not true," said Matt matter-of-factly, although he wasn't sure of any such thing.

"You think?" said Anna dubiously. "Well, explain this then – on my break today, I ran round to the stationer's on the High Street and I saw Sonja on the other side of the road. So I waved at her and I'm sure she saw me, but it was as if she pretended she hadn't!"

"Well, she probably *didn't* see you. She's blind as a bat, that Son."

Anna stared at Matt, who looked fidgety. She knew as well as he did that there was nothing wrong with Sonja's eyesight. Like so much else about her physically, it was perfect.

"She hasn't said anything to you, has she?" Anna quizzed her boyfriend. "About all this business with Ollie?"

"No!" snorted Matt, laughing a little too loudly.

He wasn't too hot on keeping secrets, but Matt couldn't see what good it would do to tell Anna what Sonja's attitude towards her was right now – it would just upset her too much.

And, deep down, Matt suspected he knew

exactly why Sonja had taken against Anna so easily – and he wasn't about to tell Anna *that* either. It was due, he was sure, to the fact that Anna hadn't been particularly enthusiastic about her big brother Owen and her friend Sonja moving in together come September. It wasn't that Anna was being moralistic, Matt knew, it was just that she thought they were rushing things

"I think they're brilliant together, Son and Owen," Anna had confided in him one night. "But why can't Sonja just think about getting a student flat-share when she moves up north and take it slowly? Why do they have to move in together so quickly? It could spoil everything between them..."

Matt had shrugged and agreed that his girlfriend had a point, but it was hard for him to listen to that and then hear Sonja's comments on the subject. "What is it with Anna, Matt? Kerry and everyone seem really excited for me and Owen, but I just get the feeling that Anna doesn't approve of us moving in together," Sonja had told him at The Loud's gig at the Railway Tavern one night a couple of weeks previously. "She's hardly said anything about it to me. Does she think I'm going to lead her beloved brother astray?"

"Don't be stupid!" Matt had laughed at her, trying to dispel the idea from his friend's head.

Right now, Matt felt sick with keeping in secrets. More than anything, he wished all the tension and bad vibes would just disappear and they could all get back to normal.

"Are you OK? You look a bit funny," asked Anna.

"Yeah... I'm – I'm just thinking that you probably don't have the energy to come along and keep me company at this gig I'm doing tonight."

Well done – good cover-up! he praised himself.

At the same time, even though it was just an excuse, he was disappointed that he'd have to go on his own to DJ at tonight's engagement party. He vaguely knew the guy whose party it was and had been looking forward to showing Anna off.

"Sorry, Matt – after the week I've had, the most energetic thing I can bear to do tonight is press 'play' on my video. I just fancy sticking on those old *Friends* tapes Kerry lent me and having a laugh."

Poor Anna, thought Matt as he bent over and kissed her forehead. She hasn't had much of a laugh the last few days – and certainly not with her 'friends'...

• • •

"Well, phone him, if you think it'll help!"

"I dunno..." shrugged Ollie, leaning his bum against the seat of his Vespa, which was parked outside Kerry's house.

"Come on, Ollie! It can't do any harm!"

Kerry looked at him pleadingly, her arms folded across her chest as the chilly evening breeze brushed over her bare arms.

"I suppose. I mean, Matt's closest to Anna just now. He'll be able to help, won't he? Put in a word for me and that?"

"Of course!" Kerry assured him.

She was starting to get desperate – she'd encourage Ollie to do anything if it helped improve the situation between him and Anna. At the moment it seemed to be getting worse and threatening to spread out and divide everyone in the crowd, if Sonja and Joe were anything to go by.

From what Ollie's said, thought Kerry, attempting to smile positively at her troubled boyfriend, *it just sounds like Joe's trying to play fair. But there's no telling Ollie that, not while he's in this martyrish mood, after having to drop out of the competition.*

Sonja was a different matter – she genuinely seemed to be outraged at the unfairness of what had happened. Kerry was totally taken aback at how angry her best friend had seemed about the whole situation. But then, like her cousin Cat, Sonja could be pretty hot-headed when she wanted to.

And then Sonja's got that weird idea that Anna's against her and Owen living together, Kerry suddenly realised. *That's what could really be making her mad at Anna...*

"You're right. I'll phone Matt when I get home – I'll have time before I have to help down in the bar and that way I should catch him before he goes off to that party he's DJing at tonight."

Kerry shivered and not just with the cold.

"Hey, Kez," said Ollie gently, sensing her mood and reaching out to give her a hug. "I know you're upset and I feel rotten too. But it'll all get sorted out..."

At that moment, with her arms wrapped around his neck, there was no way Kerry could see what Ollie was doing behind her back...

• • •

Ollie put his hand on the white-tiled wall and let the full force of the power-shower pummel him.

How did everything get this complicated? he wondered, blinking as the water coursed into his eyes.

Phoning Matt just now hadn't helped at all. Keeping his fingers crossed when he'd been hugging Kerry obviously hadn't worked either.

"Hey, Matt – where are you?" he'd said, hearing the muffled roar of traffic in the earpiece.

"I'm just outside Central Sounds. I've had to hire an amp from them for this gig I'm doing tonight."

Matt sounded a bit distant, thought Ollie. Loyalty to Anna, he supposed. Still, he and Matt were great mates, so it was worth a try...

"Yeah, I remembered you were working tonight. Uh, Matt – I was kind of hoping for a favour."

"Oh, yeah?"

"You don't think you could, well, have a word with Anna, could you? See if you could persuade her to give me time off just this once? I was thinking, maybe I could work a couple of hours in the morning before we go up to the city or—"

"Ollie, can I ask you something?" interrupted Matt.

"Um, sure..."

"Did you bad-mouth Anna to Sonja?"

"What? No! What are you on about?"

"It's just that Sonja gave me a bit of an earful on Thursday. Seemed like she thought Anna was the Wicked Witch of the West or something for screwing up your chances at this competition."

"What? Well, she didn't hear it from *me* like that! I mean, Kez probably filled her in on what was going on, but it's not as if Kez would put it like *that...*"

Ollie knew he was waffling, but what Matt had told him had really thrown him. What was Sonja playing at? She maybe sympathised with him, but she wasn't helping his cause by bitching to Matt about his own girlfriend.

"I'll have to go, Ol – I'm late," Matt had concluded their conversation in a flat voice.

So does that mean he believed me about Sonja? Ollie wondered, not even noticing that the water had begun to run cooler. *Well, one thing's for sure – he's definitely not going to help me out with persuading Anna...*

Ollie yanked the pressure control round and switched the shower off.

Suddenly the huge wave of disappointment that had been threatening to engulf him all week burst over him and Ollie thumped hard on the tiles with the side of his fist, letting out a stream of swear words into the bargain.

"This could have been it! This competition could have been the start of everything for the band!" he grumbled aloud once the worst of his frustration had ebbed away.

Then he stopped dead, only dimly aware of the throbbing pain shooting through the hand that had been hammering on the wall.

"Sorry, Anna," he said with an edge of defiance in his voice, "but I can't miss out on this, whatever you say, whatever happens. There's no *way* I can give up on my one big chance..."

CHAPTER 15

ANNA'S SMASHING TIME

Anna stared down at the cover of the book on the table and tapped it thoughtfully with her index finger.

She looked again at the page she'd been studying last night: *20 Ways To Make A Bad Situation Better* said the heading above a long list of points. Anna had dug out the book – *Improve Your Life Today* – from a pile of similarly titled paperbacks that were crammed on her small bookshelf.

3. Start a new week with a fresh approach... 11. Do something nice for someone: it'll make you feel good... 18. Take a chance on someone – you could be surprised... 20. Tell yourself you're going to have a good day and you will...

Grabbing her hairbrush from the table, Anna

brushed her long, straight brown hair back into a ponytail while rereading the four points that had struck home with her.

"Right," she announced aloud, rolling a towelling hairband off her wrist and securing her hair. "Monday it is, so let's have a fresh start!"

Glancing over into the small mirror on the wall, she practised her cheeriest smile.

"I *am* going to have a good day!" Anna said determinedly, hoping she wasn't telling herself a big fat lie.

• • •

"All right, Anna?" said Ollie, coming through from the kitchen, where he'd let himself in through the back door.

"Yes, good thanks, Ollie," Anna smiled as she opened up the café and welcomed the first two customers of the day.

Well, maybe it is *going to be a better day*, she mused, scribbling down the orders for egg and bacon breakfasts. *Ollie looks and sounds pretty cheery! And he's going to sound a lot more cheery when he hears what I've got to say...*

"And no tomatoes. I told that big bloke who works in here last time and I *still* got tomatoes. And don't make the eggs too runny. And make it a strong tea – none of your usual weak stuff. And get me another fork – this one looks dirty."

Anna smiled brightly at the fussy customer – nothing was going to dampen her spirits today. She'd had enough gloom and doom to last her a year. Enough was enough.

"Certainly," she beamed and made her way towards the kitchen.

Swooping behind the counter, she couldn't help smiling to herself.

11. Do something nice for someone: it'll make you feel good... she said to herself. *Well, here goes!*

"Was that the 'no tomatoes, no runny eggs, no manners' bloke I heard there?" Ollie grinned at her, grabbing the order out of her outstretched hand.

"Yes – he hasn't been in for a while, has he?" laughed Anna. Instantly, she slapped her hand across her mouth in case she'd been too loud – but a quick peek back through the doorway into the café showed that the man was too busy yakking to his mate to hear.

"Tell you what – you should ask him if he likes music."

Anna watched as Ollie slapped some bacon under the grill and wondered what he was on about.

"Music?" she said dubiously, thinking that

Ollie was referring to the radio station she'd tuned in to this morning.

"Yeah! Maybe you should remind him that there's a great record shop next door. Tell him the staff are very helpful."

Finally, Anna got it. It was Monday – Matt's day for running Slick Riffs – alone.

"Have you got George Michael's last album? No, *not* the covers album! I didn't *say* covers, did I? No, the one *before* that!" Ollie barked, mimicking the rude customer's blunt way of talking.

"Mmm, well, I don't think I'd wish that bloke on anyone in a hurry, specially not Matt today," smiled Anna, her spirits rising as she saw how normal and nice Ollie was being. "He's nervous enough, with the responsibility of Nick leaving him in charge all by himself."

A silence suddenly fell between them with only the popping of the bacon under the grill to break it. Anna hadn't meant for her words to come out that way – she didn't want to remind Ollie that Matt was busy doing the job that *he* normally did.

Feeling momentarily flustered, Anna stepped back and peered out into the café – but as she already knew from the absence of any bell tinkling above the front door, there were no other customers to see to as yet.

"Funny, isn't it?" said Ollie softly. "You and Matt, both being in charge..."

"Listen, Ollie," said Anna quickly, feeling her cheeks redden slightly at the awkwardness of the situation. "I just wanted to tell you something. It's just... well, I've been thinking..."

"Uh-huh?" he replied, his eyes as wide and hopeful as a child's.

"It's just that I – I think you *should* do the Battle of the Bands thing. I mean, I fixed it – you *can* have Saturday off."

"*Really?!*" said Ollie, so excited that he didn't notice the slight smell of burning coming from under the grill. "But how will you manage? Irene hasn't changed her mind, has she?"

Anna took a deep breath, pictured point number 18 on the list in her book – *Take a chance on someone – you could be surprised...* – and hoped she wasn't about to make a huge mistake.

"It's not Irene, Ol. It's, um, just that Cat's going to come in and help out."

"*Cat*!" Ollie exclaimed incredulously. "*Cat*? Didn't she once come into the kitchen and say how great it was that Nick let us watch the telly while we worked – when she was pointing at the microwave? And does she realise that aprons don't come in designer labels?!"

"Don't..." Anna groaned, rolling her eyes. "I'm

trying not to think about this too much or I might just panic and change my mind. Just shut up and be grateful."

"Course I'm grateful! In fact, I'm *this* grateful!" said Ollie enthusiastically, rushing over to Anna and scooping her up in a bear hug.

"Ollie! Put me down!" squealed Anna. "And look at the grill – the bacon's burning!"

"Uh-oh," muttered Ollie, putting her down and rushing over to try and salvage the breakfasts.

Anna smoothed her apron back down after her unexpected cuddle and did a quick check out front again.

"So, will it be all right with the competition people?" she asked Ollie, who was throwing out the burnt rashers and starting again.

"Huh?" blinked Ollie, glancing round at her.

"Well, with you pulling out; telling them you couldn't come. Will it be OK just to tell them you want your place back in the finals?"

At her question, Ollie shrugged and looked a little shamefaced.

"Well... I hadn't *actually* cancelled it with them..."

Anna blinked for a second, her feeling of *bonhomie* beginning to evaporate.

Still, I guess you can't blame him for not getting around to phoning and letting them know

The Loud were pulling out, she reasoned to herself. *Sweet as he is, he's just a typical boy, after all; burying his head in the sand and hoping it'll all magically be all right.*

"Well, at least you'll be able to tell the rest of the boys now that it's all back on," she said cheerily, trying to hang on to her positive vibes.

"Aha– ha– harummphhhh..."

The strange grunting noise Ollie had just made was *supposed* – Anna realised – to be some kind of a laugh. Only it wasn't very convincing. And the embarrassed expression on his face didn't exactly scream 'funny' either.

"Ollie?" she ventured, frowning ever so slightly. "What's up?"

"It's just— ah, hell, I'm no good at lying, Anna," said Ollie, dropping his head to one side and looking at her pleadingly. "Truth is, I already phoned Joe, Billy and Andy yesterday and told them it was all back on."

"*What*?" yelped Anna, unable to believe what she was hearing.

"Well, I just figured that we could get around it somehow – that something would come up," Ollie babbled, "and hey – look! It has! So everything's OK, isn't it? Isn't it?"

Out at the front, the awkward customer and his friend stopped their conversation mid-flow as the almighty clatter of a plate smashing vibrated from the kitchen.

"Runny eggs... weak tea... waitress who drops plates... that's it. Next time, we find a *new* café for breakfast," muttered Mr Grouch.

CHAPTER 16

MAYA'S MIND WORKS OVERTIME

"And then she threw a plate at him!"

Kerry hadn't even attempted to pin back her overenthusiastic curls this particular Tuesday afternoon – they sprung out to the side and dangled prettily around her neck as she recounted her story to Maya. She was so caught up in what she was saying that she was only dimly aware of Marcus the Siamese cat lazily reaching up and pawing at the longest tendril from the comfort of her lap.

"Wait!" said Maya, holding up her hand and interrupting Kerry's account of what had happened between Ollie and Anna the day before. "*Anna* threw a plate at *Ollie*? Are we talking about the same Anna? 'Cause the Anna I know wouldn't hurt a fly, even one that was coming at her with a machine gun!"

"Well, she didn't exactly *throw* it," said Kerry, retracting her tale. "It more kind of *fell*, when she waved her arm to one side and knocked it off the work surface. But she *was* screaming at him!"

Distracted from the conversation, Maya suddenly bolted upright from the chair by her desk, stretched her long slim neck and turned her head in the direction of the ringing phone.

Kerry stayed schtum, watching her friend and wondering what it was that had gripped her attention so much. It also occurred to her that Maya – frozen in that particular position – reminded her of a meerkat she and her kid brother Lewis had ogled at in a zoo a couple of years back.

"Mayyyyyyaaaaaaaaa! It's for yoooooooo!" came the call from downstairs, in the lilting Irish voice of Brigid, who looked after the Joshi children – though Maya, with her 27-year-old boyfriend, hardly included herself in that statistic – until their parents got home from work.

"Back in a sec, Kez," said Maya, scooting quickly out of her bedroom.

"No problem. Oh, *ye-oww*WWW!"

Kerry's head jerked to the side as Marcus finally got hold of the temptingly dangling curl and pulled hard with his claws.

• • •

"Hello?"

Maya didn't know why she said that and in such a 'who-is-this?' tone – Brigid had already mouthed to her that it was Alex on the line. But something inside was making her hold back; just like she felt he was holding something back from *her*.

"Maya, it's me. How's it going?"

"Hi, Alex. Yes, I'm fine."

No I'm not, she corrected herself silently. *I'm not fine. I'm the one who's always doling out advice to my friends and here I am, completely confused about how to handle what's going on in my own relationship!*

"Hey – one more exam tomorrow and then you're back out in the real world!"

"Yes, I suppose so."

"Bet you can't wait!"

"Mmm."

"I know I can't!"

"Uh-huh."

"So... how's the studying going?"

"It's all right."

"Not doing your head in then?"

"No, not too much."

"Maya – is something up?"

"No," she lied. "Why, should there be?"

"I don't know – you just don't sound like you. In fact, you sounded like this when I spoke to you on Saturday too."

"Well, I was fine then and I'm fine now."

"It's just that this is going to be a pretty short conversation if we carry on like this..."

Maybe it wouldn't be if you gave me a clue about what's really happening with you and Holly, thought Maya treacherously, gripping the phone so hard her knuckles were white.

After Sonja's revelation the previous Friday, Maya had been desperate to hear from Alex. To hear his explanation of why he'd taken his ex to the Railway Tavern without even telling her he planned to do it. That's what really bothered Maya; at a pinch, she could just about have coped with Alex taking an old flame out, but only for a very good reason and only if she knew it was happening in advance. The fact that he'd said nothing to her made the whole situation reek of secrecy.

Although how could that be? she'd tried to reason with herself on Friday evening, awaiting the familiar teatime call from her boyfriend. *If Alex wanted to be secretive about Holly then he wouldn't take her to a place that's full of my friends...*

But if she was starting to doubt her own worries and see them as over-reaction on her part, they soon returned tenfold as the hours dragged by and the phone never rang. Pure pride had stopped her from picking up the phone herself and dialling Alex's number.

It had taken till Saturday lunchtime for him to call: bright and breezy and full of apologies about getting caught up at a work's leaving do that started when the college closed for the evening and carried on into the night. When it came to explaining Holly, Alex told Maya that she'd phoned him out of the blue on Thursday night, saying she was bored and could she tag along to see this band he'd been banging on about at the house party earlier in the week.

"'Course, I hadn't planned on going, since you were stuck at home," Alex had said casually. "But then I thought, why not? Maya wouldn't want me to miss out on seeing The Loud just 'cause *she* couldn't!"

You want a bet? Maya had thought, listening to his words.

And that was it, as far as discussion about Holly went. No matter how Maya had tried subtly to push him during that conversation on Saturday, he'd resorted to bland, non-informative scraps about the evening; how Holly thought the band was great, especially the slow numbers; how Matt seemed to be distracted and kept messing up the sound.

None of what he said fulfilled Maya's need to know how they got on together; whether Holly was as attractive to him as she once was; whether he was as attractive to her as he once was; how they left each other at the end of the night. Did they agree to go out together again? Did he give her a kiss, even just a so-called friendly one?

It was these kind of questions that had rattled through Maya's mind the last few days, making her more resentful and less chatty every time he called.

"Maya? Are you still there?"

"Yes," said Maya, coming out of her reverie.

"Are you sure you're all right? Has something happened with your parents over the last couple of days? Has Sunny upset you again and you just can't speak about it on the phone?"

Can't you understand that it's you that's upsetting me? And if you can't sense that, then maybe you're not the person I thought you were...

"Alex, I'm OK. Look, I've got to go..."

"Listen – you'll be back at photography club tomorrow, won't you? And we can go out together after that and talk about whatever's bothering you. All right?"

Maya felt overcome by a wave of irritation; he was talking to her like a teacher, not a boyfriend.

"Right. Well, I've got to go. Speak to you later."

With his startled "Uh, bye!" still ringing in her ears, Maya stomped back upstairs, her head thumping with images of him and this faceless girl together. This girl he had so much in common with.

After all, she thought bitterly, her hand thudding down on the banister, *they have the same group of friends, similar jobs, are round about the same age...*

From the corner of her eye, Maya saw the door of Sunny's room move slightly and heard a floorboard in her sister's room creak. Sunny was obviously up to her usual tricks, listening at the door for any juicy titbits. But Maya was too down to care much.

Pushing open the door to her own room, Maya gave a little gasp; she'd totally forgotten that Kerry had come round to visit her.

Or rather offload her worries – which Maya just wasn't in the mood for all of a sudden.

"Was that Alex?" asked Kerry, trying not to wince as Marcus purred contentedly and kneaded her thigh with his needle-sharp claws.

"Yes," nodded Maya, going back over to her seat at the book-strewn desk.

"What's he saying?"

"Nothing much," Maya shrugged.

"Is he missing you?"

"Don't know."

"Oh."

Kerry looked a little put out at Maya's sudden coolness. Like the rest of the crowd, she felt in awe of Maya at the best of times, and in the rare moments when Maya seemed to be in a bad mood, she was almost intimidating, especially to someone as easily ruffled as Kerry.

In the face of Maya's mood change, Kerry wondered if she shouldn't just make her excuses and leave. But Maya had seemed quite pleased to see her when she'd first arrived and, after all, Kerry really wanted her friend's opinion and advice on the Ollie and Anna situation. So she decided to take up where she left off before Maya's phone call had taken her away.

"Anyway, like I was saying, I don't think Ollie meant anything by accepting the place in the finals behind Anna's back. He was just so desperate to be at that comp—"

"Kez, doing *anything* behind someone's back is totally out of order. It's just about the nastiest thing anyone could do to a person!" snapped Maya, muddling up her own problems and fears with what was going on in her mates' lives.

"But Ollie wouldn't deliberately set out to hurt anyone!"

"Maybe... maybe not," shrugged Maya. "Listen, Kerry, I've got a pile of work to get on with."

Kerry was taken aback. She had, she realised, just been dismissed.

Lifting Marcus from her lap – by carefully loosening a couple of his claws from his grip on her jeans – Kerry hurriedly got up to leave.

"I'd better go..." she said in a small, breathy voice, before grabbing her jacket and scurrying out of the room.

Angry at Alex and angry at herself for not knowing what to do and taking it out on poor Kerry, Maya picked up the nearest book and hurled it at the wall, where its spine cracked, sending reams of pages fluttering down on to her bed.

And, unlike Anna and the plate, there was no mistaking Maya's raging outburst as purely accidental.

CHAPTER 17

HEALING HANDS

Anna glanced over automatically as the bell above the café door tinkled into life.

"Hi," said Sonja without any warmth in her voice as she breezed over towards where Anna stood, taking a couple of customers' orders.

Uh-oh, thought Anna, checking out her friend's unsmiling face.

"Hi, Sonja. I'll be with you in a second," she replied, turning back to complete her order.

"Don't bother. I'm just after Ollie. Is he through in the back?"

"Um, no," said Anna, trying to ignore the edge in Sonja's voice and finish scribbling on her pad. "It's his turn for a late shift. He won't be in till eleven."

"Well, could you give him a message, please?"

"Sorry about this," Anna apologised to the two women at the table. "OK, Sonja, what is it?"

"Tell him to give me a ring and let me know what the arrangements are for Saturday."

Anna blinked at her stony-faced friend, who looked every inch the ice maiden with her Scandinavian blonde looks and frosty expression. She was obviously talking about the Battle of the Bands competition.

"All right, Sonja, I'll tell him," she nodded, turning her attention back to her customers. "And did you want any bread with that?"

"Yes, that would be—"

"Yeah, you see, I want to be there on such an important day for the lads," Sonja interrupted in barbed tones. "*And* I want to show Ollie that *some* of his friends support what he's doing!"

The two women stared after Sonja as she flounced out of the End, but Anna kept her gaze resolutely glued to her order pad.

This, she thought, the penned words on her order pad dancing in front of her eyes, *is getting too much...*

• • •

Anna's hand hovered over the phone then flopped back down in her lap.

Thinking about it, she didn't want to call Matt and burden him with what had happened with Sonja. He was wound up enough by the situation and she'd had a hard job persuading him not to make an issue of it, and not to pull out of his band commitments, either at tomorrow's regular Thursday night gig or at Saturday's competition. Much as she appreciated his support in all this, Anna didn't see any benefit in putting more of a chasm between them all.

Suddenly, she remembered that he was working tonight anyway, DJing at a birthday party in a country hotel a few miles away.

"Maybe Owen," she murmured to herself, thinking of her faraway brother. His easygoing assurances were bound to make her feel better.

Her hand reached out for the phone once more, but she snatched it back again.

"Hey, Anna, why are you sounding so down?" she said aloud, imagining how their conversation would go.

"Well, I'm down because your girlfriend Sonja, who you love very much, was a bit of a bitch to me today!" she answered herself.

Anna flopped back down on her sofa and sighed. What was going to happen? Was her network of friends all going to break up? Did this spell the end of everything?

Maybe I'll have to give up my job... she mused miserably. *Ollie is Nick's nephew after all, so if things just keep getting worse and worse, it'll have to be me who leaves. And then, of course, I'd have to give up my flat...*

Hot, self-pitying tears prickled uncharacteristically in Anna's eyes as her imagination ran away with her and spelt out the worst-case scenario. The flat was so precious to Anna; it was tiny, but it was her own little bolt-hole, her security blanket, and she hadn't been able to believe her luck when she'd landed in Winstead and found herself a job that included accommodation.

The thought of having that snatched away from her was too upsetting to contemplate.

"Yooo-hoo!" came a call at the front door, accompanied by a sudden ring of the bell. "It's only me! Cat!"

Anna leapt to her feet. She was normally very self-reliant, but right now, it was lovely to hear a friendly voice.

"Hi, honey!" said Cat, bounding in and enveloping Anna in a big hug.

Anna tried hard not to cough at Cat's overwhelming cloud of perfume.

"It's great to see you, Cat. But what are you doing over this way?"

"I'm here to help," Cat beamed, a wide, redlipsticked grin on her face. "So get your clothes off."

"What?"

"You heard. Strip!" giggled Cat, relishing her friend's stunned expression.

• • •

"Oooooohhhh..."

"Is that the spot?"

"Yep. Owww..."

"You've got a real knot of muscles there, Ms Michaels. It's a case of too much work and too much stress!"

"Tell me about it..." mumbled Anna as Cat massaged her back.

"Never mind. I'm here to help!" trilled Cat, stopping to warm more aromatherapy oil between her hands. "A free therapeutic massage for you tonight and then I'll be at your beck and call all day Saturday!"

"Thanks, Cat," said Anna dreamily, relaxing for the first time in ages. "I really needed this..."

"Thank your darling boyfriend. He's the one that rang and asked me to come over and cheer you up."

Anna, lying tummy-down on a fluffy towel-covered mat and naked apart from her white cotton knickers, smiled to herself. Matt really was proving to be a very thoughtful boyfriend – seeing to her welfare even when he wasn't around himself to help.

Mind you, I suppose he thought Cat would just come round for a chat, Anna mused. *He probably didn't reckon on her using me as a guinea pig for one of the treatments she's learned on her Beauty Course...*

"You know," said Cat, moving her hands in firm but gentle circles either side of Anna's spine, "I still can't believe you didn't fill me in about Ollie when you asked me to come in and do his shift. I mean, the cheek of him! Already planning to go to the competition anyway!"

"I know. But that's not what's really bothering me about all this."

"Then what is?"

"Well, it's part of the reason I didn't say anything when I phoned you and took you up on your offer to help in the caff: I hate the way everyone seems to be taking sides..."

"Like who?" asked Cat, still feeling out of the loop with her friends, what with their exams and her own college commitments.

"There's Matt for a start – he's so annoyed with Ollie for my sake. And I guess Kerry is probably on Ollie's side for *his* sake. Then there's the lads in the band – Andy and Billy are both leaning towards Ollie, understandably, because this competition could be really big for them all. But Matt says that Joe's had a bit of a run-in with Ollie, because he sees *my* side of things."

"Ah, Joe! What a sweetie!" cooed Cat.

"I know, but I don't want any of this stuff between Ollie and me making things bad between the two of them. They're such old friends!"

"But Ollie's being a selfish git!" proclaimed Cat righteously. "And I should know – I've been a selfish git myself at times!"

Anna closed her eyes and smiled again at Cat's very astute assessment of herself.

Still, it's funny that I used to think of Cat and Sonja as so different, thought Anna, reflecting on the year or so she'd known Cat, her cousin and the others. *But there are times when Cat is as friendly and kind as Sonja usually is, and Sonja can be as monstrous as Cat at her worst...*

"So what about Maya? What's she got to say about all this stuff? And what about my darling cousin? I bet *she's* not short of an opinion..."

Anna gulped. She hadn't wanted to get into this. It could only do what she dreaded most – make the sides issue more obvious.

"Um, well, I don't know about Maya. She's hasn't been around much."

"Of course. Her mum and dad'll still have her

chained to her desk studying," laughed Cat. "And what about Sonja?"

Anna gave an involuntary shiver at the memory of Sonja's terse words downstairs that morning.

"Oh, are you cold? Will I bring the heater over?" asked Cat with concern.

"No, I'm fine."

"Well, if you're sure. So what about Sonja then?" Cat returned to her question, not easily deflected from her theme.

Anna thought for a second and then decided that if Cat went along to the Railway Tavern as usual tomorrow night, she was going to find out her cousin's opinion pretty quickly anyway.

"Sonja seems to think I've, um, been a bit harsh on Ollie, what with the competition being so important and everything," Anna explained, trying to opt for the least inflammatory version of events.

It didn't work.

"What? How dare she! Wait till I have a word with *her*!" exclaimed Cat angrily.

Anna bit her lip and tried not to yelp as Cat's fingers dug agonisingly into her tender muscles.

CHAPTER 18

BATTLEZONE

Ollie marvelled at his ability to do two things simultaneously.

He remembered when he'd first become aware he could do it. At secondary school, his history teacher was one of the old-fashioned types, who often dictated pages and pages of facts for his pupils to scribble into their jotters. That's when Ollie found he had the amazing ability to copy down everything, word perfect, while disengaging his brain and daydreaming about who'd be up for a game of footie at breaktime.

Now he was doing it again, singing one of The Loud's tunes up on the stage of the Railway Tavern, without any of the audience realising that his mind was preoccupied with anything but the lyrics.

Once we get this competition out of the way on Saturday, I'll fix it with everyone, he promised himself. *Anna, obviously, and Joe too. I need to have a talk with Matt as well and get things sorted.*

He glanced over at the mixing desk and saw that Matt was still looking as sour as if he'd sucked a jug of lemon juice through a straw. He'd arrived – late – with that expression on his face and only ten minutes to spare before the band were due to go on stage.

Mind you, I'm just grateful he showed up at all, thought Ollie, effortlessly launching into the chorus.

Matt had been ominously quiet all week, never showing his face in the End, and when Ollie had tried to phone him a couple of times, all he'd got was the answering service on Matt's mobile and he'd never returned Ollie's calls.

Ollie had had to resort to asking Anna if Matt had heard his messages, which outlined the plans for Saturday's competition. That had been hard to do: Ollie and Anna had kept communication to the bare minimum over the last few days – "Is that order ready?", "Yes – there it is", "Thanks" – and stretching it any further had seemed excruciatingly hard.

Ollie hated acting like this – he was a born

chatterer – but he knew that he'd annoyed Anna so much that the best thing was to shut up, stay quiet and not risk winding her up any further.

That stiff only-talking-when-you-need-to rule was applying to his relationship with Joe too. His best mate was still acting really uptight and snappy with him, and even though Joe was still suffering from the remnants of flu, it didn't seem to Ollie that there was any reason for him to be that way.

Maybe he's broken up with Meg! it suddenly occurred to Ollie. *But he's really into her... But what if she's chucked him? That would explain his weird grumpiness. Maybe he doesn't want to tell anyone yet. That would be very Joe...*

Ollie made a mental note to be more understanding to Joe, just in case his guess was correct. And, at the moment, that was the best Ollie could do. He was so stressed out about the competition – especially with all the organising he had to do since the band's manager, Nick, was too many thousands of miles away to be of any help – that he didn't have his normal boundless supply of energy to deal with everything at once.

And, apart from the problems that were affecting him directly, there was more hassle brewing for another one of the crowd. According to Billy and Andy, something was up with Maya and Alex. Maya hadn't shown up at photography club the previous evening, even though her exams were out of the way. Alex had apparently been asking the two lads if they'd seen or heard from her and had seemed pretty wound up about it.

I wonder if Maya will turn up here tonight? thought Ollie, his gaze moving round the room in search of the comforting vision of his girlfriend. Kerry had said that Maya was very off with her when she'd popped round to see her on Tuesday. *If I had time, I'd phone Maya myself and see if she's OK. Well, that's another thing that'll have to be on next week's sorting-out-the-world list...*

At last he spotted Kerry, but he wasn't as comforted by what he saw as he'd hoped to be. Kerry looked tense and with good reason. Sitting next to her at the small table were two squabbling girls: Sonja and her cousin Cat seemed to be hissing like vipers at each other.

Please don't let that be anything about the me and Anna bust-up, Ollie prayed silently.

But deep down he already knew that was *just* what it was.

• • •

"Can't wait to hear what Nick's been up to, can you?" guffawed Derek.

"Yeah, yeah!" Ollie chuckled, wishing he could wriggle away from the conversation he'd been trapped in since The Loud got off stage. But he couldn't exactly; after all, Derek was the pub landlord as well as the guy who let them play this regular spot.

"Oh, sorry, Ollie lad – got to go. The missus is calling me over," Derek suddenly excused himself, nodding over towards the woman behind the bar with the astounding collection of gold chains draped round her neck.

"All right, Eva?" Ollie called across, giving the woman a quick wave while silently thanking her for getting him out a dull situation.

I'll find Kerry and say hello, Ollie decided, turning and making his way through the crowded bar, *and then I'll catch Matt and tell him in more detail about what's happening on Saturday.*

"Hey, gorgeous!" he said to Kerry, spotting her before she saw him on her way to the loo.

"Hi, Ollie – wow, am I glad to see you!" she smiled, relief written all over her face.

"Why, what's up?" he asked, though he suspected he already knew the answer.

"It's like everyone's taking sides or something!" explained Kerry, nodding back the way she'd come. "I mean, at the table just now, Sonja's sitting with Billy and Andy, bitching on about Cat—"

"I saw them arguing from the stage."

"—yeah, well, it was all this 'Anna's in the right', 'No. Ollie's in the right' stuff. It was doing my head in! And now Cat's standing over with Matt while he packs up the mixing desk and Joe's over there too!"

"Oh, no..." sighed Ollie.

"Ol – you've got to sort this out! It's just so horrible, everyone fighting like this!"

"OK, OK, I'll try," he reassured Kerry, reaching out and squeezing her hand.

Giving him a quick peck, Kerry smiled nervously and disappeared off to the loo.

"Right," muttered Ollie as he bypassed Sonja and the other lads at the table and headed directly over to Matt.

Something was going on, he noticed, seeing Cat wrap her arms around Joe.

"Good luck!" Ollie thought he heard her say as he came closer.

"Hi. What's up?" Ollie beamed, his lopsided grin as genuine and friendly as he could make it.

"Uh, nothing," murmured Joe, his cheeks looking unmistakably pink with embarrassment.

"Nothing *you'd* be interested in, Ollie Stanton since you're only interested in yourself!"

Cat's sneer was like a body blow to Ollie. He'd

been a brilliant friend to Cat in the past, giving her chance after chance when a lot of other people wouldn't – even the time when her jealousy had made her try and split him and Kerry up. And now Cat seemed to have conveniently forgotten all that and was having a go at him. And when Cat decided to have a go, Ollie knew, being on the receiving end was not a good place to be.

"Cat!" he exclaimed indignantly. "Since when have I ever—"

"Sorry – got to go. Come on, Joe," she butted in, linking her arm around a surprised-looking Joe and practically steering him away.

"Well, I didn't see that one coming!" Ollie laughed sheepishly, looking hopefully towards Matt for sympathy.

But he was looking at the wrong person.

"Well, you probably won't have seen this one coming either," said Matt, the muscles in his chiselled cheeks twitching.

"What? What are you on about?" asked Ollie, puzzled.

"You've really upset Anna this time. Cat was round at her flat last night and heard all about it," Matt growled. "So tonight, I'm going to help you shift the gear away and then that's it – count me out."

"Huh?"

"Well, I'm sorry for the sake of Joe and the other lads, but you'll have to find someone else to do your sound on Saturday, Ol, 'cause there's no way I'm doing it!"

Ollie stood rooted to the spot as Matt heaved the heavy mixing desk under one arm and headed off to the exit.

"Hi, remember me?"

Ollie stared blankly at the girl who'd appeared at his side – but at this particular moment, he couldn't do two things at once. He was too stunned by the catastrophe of Matt letting him down to go raking through his memory banks to find a name to match this face.

"I'm Holly," said the red-headed girl helpfully. "I came to see you guys last week with Alex, remember?"

"Uh, oh, yeah," spluttered Ollie, the penny dropping.

"I was just wondering, did Alex come tonight? I arrived half-way through your set, but I haven't seen him..."

"Um, no, I don't think he did," said Ollie, trying hard to think straight.

"Oh, well," shrugged Holly, looking faintly disappointed.

"Did he say he was coming?" Ollie asked, distractedly glancing over her shoulder as he saw

Matt and Joe coming back in from loading up the car.

"No, no... I just popped in on the off chance," shrugged Holly. "So... is, er, his girlfriend here then?"

"Maya? No, she's not. Maybe they're out together somewhere."

"Oh. Oh, right," Holly replied, biting at her lip edgily. "Well, I'd better go. I'm sure you've got plenty of other people to talk to!"

I wouldn't bet on it, thought Ollie, watching her walk away. *There seem to be fewer and fewer people wanting to talk to me every day at the moment...*

CHAPTER 19

TESTING TIMES

Joe shuffled slightly on the low, seventies-style vinyl seat. It made a loud, farting noise, piling embarrassment on top of the misery and nervousness he already felt.

"I still think you ought to have cancelled this driving test!" his mum had twittered as he left the house that morning. She'd been holding out his jacket to help him on with it, he remembered now with a cringe. His mum really did think he was five years old and in need of help wiping his nose sometimes.

"Mum – I *told* you," he'd moaned at her. "I've already passed my *written* driving test, so I might as well get the practical test out of the way now, while I've got the chance. I don't want it hanging over my head for months!"

Especially if I'm not even here in Winstead to sit it, he'd said to himself, thinking of the secret he'd told no one but Meg so far.

"But you're *still* not a hundred per cent over that flu and you're exhausted with all your exams," Susie Gladwin had prattled on regardless. "And Meg thinks so too. When she rang last night, I was just saying, 'Well, he might not listen to his old mum, but he might listen to you!' I don't know why you didn't give her a call when you got back in from playing at your gig!"

"Because it was *late*, Mum, and Meg has an exam herself this morning!" Joe had tried to protest. He hadn't wanted to add that he was too depressed after the atmosphere of the gig to talk to anyone anyway – even Meg.

Joe was about to wriggle into a more comfortable position, but the fear of making the orange vinyl chair fart again soon put a stop to that.

Once this competition's out of the way, I'll have to speak to Ollie, clear the air, Joe promised himself, unaware that his best mate had made a similar vow the night before. *But first, I've just got to get this test out of the way and the exam this afternoon...*

Joe glanced across the glass-topped table in the middle of the room – laden with a mound of hopelessly out-of-date magazines – and spotted that the guy in his twenties sitting in a matching farty chair opposite looked even sweatier and more nervous than he was.

"Well, just try to relax, dear," he remembered his mother's parting words that morning. "You can only do your best. And, like your exams, you can always try again another time..."

And I've got to be nicer to Mum, Joe told himself. *She irritates me sometimes, but she's been really sweet and all I've done is grouch at her the last couple of weeks. I'll have to buy her some flowers or maybe that Shania Twain CD she's always singing along to on the radio...*

"Joe Gladwin? Ah, Mr Gladwin – I'm Mr Antonio and I'll be your examiner for today. Could you follow me, please?"

Joe nodded at the grey-haired man, gulped and rose out of the chair with a final fart.

I'm sure I'll laugh about this later, Joe told himself, feeling more tense than he had done for a long, long time.

• • •

Anna noisily clattered dirty plates on to her tray, but Ollie didn't seem to get the hint.

"Aw, that's too bad. Well, what about Dylan?

Hasn't he ever done sound engineering for bands? Yeah? Great – sure I'll wait."

Anna stared hard at the back of Ollie's head, willing him to realise that he was trying her patience that little bit too much. But all Ollie did was scrabble about in his jeans' pocket for more change to feed the wall phone.

The café door tinkled open and a couple of middle-aged women came in, loaded down with shopping bags.

"Be with you in a sec!" Anna called over to them in an unnecessarily loud voice, hoping to catch Ollie's attention and prick his conscience.

It didn't work.

"Yeah, Dylan? Did Steve explain what I'm after? Yeah – that's right. It's short notice, I know, but Matt can't do this competition tomorrow. I mean, it's going to be great, it really is. And you know Andy? Our bass player? Yeah, the skinny one with black hair. His cousin's going to drive us there; we've hired a minibus and everything. You would? Wow! That's brilliant! But you normally work Saturdays, don't you? Won't your boss... Will he? Well, *you're* lucky! I practically had to beg..."

Ollie's voice trailed off as he realised what he'd said and he turned round cautiously to see if Anna was within listening range. Which, of course, she was.

Anna gave him a withering look, clattered the remaining debris of the table on to her tray and stomped off to the kitchen, furious at Ollie's disregard for her and his work. Since ten o'clock that morning, he'd spent half his time glued to the phone instead of serving or cooking, finalising arrangements for the next day's big event. It was driving Anna round the bend.

"Oh, hello, Dorothy," she managed to smile, coming through into the kitchen and finding the two older women who worked there standing with their coats on, furtively gossiping.

"Hello, dear," said Dorothy, slipping out of her camel-hair coat as she got ready to start her shift, while Irene did the opposite and pulled her raincoat on.

"You two look suspicious," Anna joked, noting their awkward silence at her approach.

"Anna, could Dorothy and I have a quick word?"

"Well, there's customers just arrived," said Anna, pointing her thumb over her shoulder back out in the direction of the front café, "and I'd better see to them since Ollie's as good as useless this morning..."

"Anna – that's what we want to talk about."

Anna stopped mid-rant, seeing Irene's determined expression.

"What's wrong?" she asked, her eyes flicking from one woman to the other.

"Anna, we both know there's this atmosphere between you and Ollie at the moment," Dorothy, the plumper of the two women, began.

"And we're not here to say who's right and who's wrong," chipped in Irene.

"But Irene and I really aren't happy working in these conditions. Especially since Irene feels partly to blame."

"What with me going off to my brother's golden wedding and causing that row between you..."

"Irene!" exclaimed Anna, "Please don't think like that! It wasn't your fault! Please don't think for a second—"

"Anna, dear," interrupted Dorothy, holding her hand up. "Whatever the ins and outs, we just wanted to tell you that we've both decided something."

"What? What are you talking about?" asked Anna, her heart pounding with anticipation.

The ladies exchanged looks before Dorothy spoke again.

"Anna, we're both terribly fond of you and Ollie. But this can't go on. We won't be saying anything about it to Nick, but if you and Ollie don't get this sorted out..."

Dorothy paused, sending Anna's heart racing.

"If you two don't get this sorted out," Irene leapt in, "then I'm afraid we'll have to hand our notice in."

Anna felt her blood run cold.

When Nick had gone away, he'd been furious enough at the fact that his battered, worthless old radio had vanished off the premises. How angry was he going to be once he found out that his two oldest, most loyal members of staff had vanished too?

CHAPTER 20

WHAT A PERFORMANCE!

"Ta-*NAAaaaaa*! Here I am! Ready for action!"

Cat stood in the doorway of the End, arms flung wide, one knee artfully bent inward in the pose of a true performer.

Anna felt the smile freeze on her face. It was worse than she'd expected.

Cat – the professional actress that she was – had obviously decided that looking the part meant you were half-way to doing a good job. Therefore, she'd turned up at ten to nine this Saturday morning in full waitress costume. But like a waitress out of an ancient *Carry On* movie...

Her hair was perfectly scraped up into a high French roll, but it looked less like an efficient work style and more like the sort of thing Patsy out of *Absolutely Fabulous* would go for. A skin-tight white

T-shirt stretched itself across her ample bosom, the whiteness of it failing miserably to hide the luminous pink of the bra she'd bizarrely chosen to wear today. Below that was a bum-skimming black velvet skirt, worn with sheer black tights.

"And look!" squealed Cat, pointing her foot. "I treated myself to these yesterday, so I'd look really smart!"

Anna nodded as she checked out the black leather wedge shoes. With their pretty ankle straps, they were undoubtedly lovely shoes, but where Cat had got the idea that brand new, four-inch high wedges were what a waitress wore was beyond her. Anna's uniform had always consisted of a simple T-shirt, jeans and the comfiest of trainers, along with her basic white apron.

"But I've got your boyfriend to thank for getting me here on time this morning," trilled Cat, beaming at a sleepy-looking Matt standing beside her. "If he hadn't surprised me and come by to pick me up, I'd have been horribly late. You've got no idea how long it takes to do this hairstyle!"

"Thanks, Matt," smiled Anna, who had been very surprised to see the rusty old mustard Lada draw up in front of the café a couple of minutes before. "Anyway, do you want to grab an apron, Cat? They're just hanging up on a hook in the kitchen."

"Oh, yes! I remember seeing them there!" giggled Cat, wobbling off behind the counter.

"Thanks," Anna repeated, giving Matt a grateful peck on the lips. "What made you decide to do that?"

"Aww, well," shrugged Matt, his dark hair uncombed and sticking up at a stupid angle at this (for him) ungodly hour on a Saturday morning. "I couldn't sleep last night – kept thinking off all the hassle you were having."

Anna nodded. When he'd come round for an hour the night before, she'd told him about Irene and Dorothy's ultimatum and also her frustration at being unable to do anything about it. It had gone on to be the most frantically busy Friday they'd ever had and she'd never had a second to talk to Ollie. Then he'd scarpered off to a final band rehearsal the instant the café shut for the night, having rushed through his kitchen-tidying duties as Anna settled up the bills with the last of the customers.

"So I just thought that the one thing I could do to help was make sure *madam* got here on time..." grinned Matt, nodding in the direction of the kitchen.

"Smart move. You're a nice guy, aren't you?" smiled Anna, reaching over to give him a hug.

"Yes, I am," yawned Matt, squeezing her

sleepily. "And don't let anyone tell you different."

"I won't," she whispered, sinking into his arms and wishing she could stay there instead of having to deal with another day at the End and whatever grief *that* might give her. Especially with Cat lending a hand...

"How does this one look? Is it cute?"

Anna smiled at Cat as she bounded through the doorway and didn't have the energy, or the inclination, to explain to her that the purpose of an apron *wasn't* to look cute.

"So, what's going to be my job today? Should I be in charge of cakes maybe?" said Cat, her glossy, pastel-pink lipstick twinkling as she spoke. "Or maybe I could just do writing things down that customers want. I could do that easily. My primary school teacher always said I was a beautiful writer. *And* speller. Or what about if I make all the milkshakes? I've always wanted to do them. How do you work milkshakes, Anna? Is there a button on this or something?"

Cat squinted at the coffee machine, searching in vain for a button that said 'milkshakes'.

"Good luck," whispered Matt, bending over to kiss Anna goodbye.

"I'll need it..." Anna whispered back...

• • •

All the participating bands had soundchecked, running through their sets before the audience and judges came in, and were nervously trying to relax back stage before the main event started at 5pm.

Not that back stage was all that comfy to relax in. *The Titanic* turned out to be the city's 'newest nightclub', transformed recently from being what everyone in the area knew to be the dodgiest nightclub in the district. And while *The Titanic* seemed to have had plenty of money spent on it out front – with glittering chrome and corny shipshape motifs splashed around – behind the scenes, the decor was as seedy as it must have been back in the days when it was still the grotty old *Mardi Gras Club*.

"What a dump!" muttered Andy, spreading an old copy of the *NME* on the floor of the corridor before he dared sit down on the dusty, cigarette-strewn floor.

"Never mind that – the good news is that the rest of the bands are all crap!" Billy whispered jubilantly to the others.

"Yeah," said Dylan, the guy from Central Sounds, Winstead's music store, who'd filled in as sound engineer in Matt's absence. "You guys are about three thousand light years better than any of the other amateurs here!"

"Brilliant!" beamed Ollie, a feeling of happiness flooding into his soul for the first time in weeks. "This is it, lads! We are on our way to a record contract!"

"But," said Joe, stopping to blow his nose hard. "There's something funny going on."

Ollie's spirits sank. Trust Joe to be the prophet of doom...

"What?" asked Billy, wide-eyed.

"I was just speaking to Chris," said Joe, referring to Andy's cousin who'd driven them to the finals. "He said that that last band—"

"Who? The guys in the orange dungarees?" snorted Ollie, remembering the pathetic vocals and even more pathetic dance routines of the wannabe boy band.

"Yeah – them," nodded Joe. "Well, apparently Chris saw their lead singer looking *very* pally with that bloke who's the main judge."

"Who is that bloke who's judging anyway?" asked Andy. "He looks like a real sad case with his designer shades and his eighties rock-star mullet..."

"Yeah and when's someone going to get round to telling us which record company's going to offer the deal?" Billy chipped in.

"I suppose they'll announce it once the competition starts properly," shrugged Ollie. "But come on, lads – don't get all bogged down in bitching about the other bands and stuff. Let's be positive and concentrate on what we're here to do. 'Cause this is the start of our future – the four of us are going places!"

But maybe not together, thought Joe bleakly as Ollie slapped him warmly on the back.

• • •

"Er, I don't mean to complain," said the woman at the table by the door. "But this isn't what I ordered..."

Anna sighed inwardly and smiled her most understanding smile at the customer.

"Sorry about that – what did you order?"

"Um, a bagel with cream cheese and salmon."

"Right..." said Anna patiently, studying the plate that contained what looked like a bagel with cream cheese and salmon. "And what's wrong with it?"

"It's just that it's not cream cheese," the woman said apologetically. "It's yoghurt."

"Yoghurt?" squeaked Anna, trying not to look too surprised.

"Yes," said the woman, lifting the top of the bitten-into bagel and pointing to something vaguely yellowy. "*Pineapple* yoghurt, I think..."

Anna glanced over to the table by the jukebox, where four lads sat transfixed as Cat took their order, her tongue stuck out in concentration and her hips unconsciously wiggling to the Blur track playing in the background.

"Sorry about that," Anna apologised, whisking the plate away. "I'll get that changed for you straightaway."

She couldn't help noticing the time on the woman's watch as she passed up her plate: it felt like six o'clock at night, but it was still only half-past ten in the morning.

It was going to be a *long* day.

• • •

"The Loud are *bound* to win."

"Really?" said Kerry, breathlessly pulling off her coat and trying to relax now that she'd found Sonja standing in the packed audience. Kerry had rushed straight from the chemist shop where she worked on Saturdays to Winstead station, and had managed to catch a train that got her to the city in time to watch The Loud's performance. "But what have I missed? What have some of the other bands been like?"

"Absolutely rubbish. But none of them have been as bad as this lot!" Sonja moaned to Kerry.

And Sonja was right – the five lads up on stage just now were plain embarrassing, bouncing around in a so-called dance routine completely out of time with each other, and miming badly to a pathetic love song.

"And somebody shoot the stylist!" Sonja moaned. "I mean, orange dungarees, for goodness' sake!"

"Son! Shut up!" Kerry pleaded. "The woman next to you could be their mum!"

"Poor woman then," sniggered Sonja. "Anyway, I'm allowed to have an opinion, aren't I?"

"Yes, but sometimes... sometimes you just come out with stuff and don't care if you hurt anybody," Kerry whispered, finally deciding it was time to stop being upset by the Anna/Ollie situation and try to do something about it.

"What's that supposed to mean?"

"Sonja, I think you've been really mean about Anna. And I think you should say sorry to Matt for slagging off his girlfriend."

"Hold on, whose side are you on? What about Ollie?" protested Sonja, while someone tutted loudly behind them.

"I'm sick of sides, Son and I'm sick of us all falling out. And I'm going to tell Ollie the same thing right after this competition's over," said Kerry, letting everything out. "It's like we've only got this summer together and then everything's bound to change, with people going off to college and university in September. It's too sad to think we might just waste our last few months as a crowd all bickering and fighting!"

"But Anna hasn't given Ollie one bit of encouragement and she's supposed to be his friend!"

"Son – are you still annoyed with Anna 'cause you think she's got a downer on you and Owen?" Kerry ventured. "Because I don't think that's true. But if you do, then you've got to talk to her and sort it out, instead of bottling it up and getting angry with her for Ollie's sake!"

Sonja folded her arms sulkily across her chest and stared off at the stage and Bad Boys Poo.

It made her miserable, being told off like that. But it made her even more miserable, realising that Kerry had a point...

• • •

"Is she new? That beautiful girl with the short skirt and big hair? Will she be here all the time?" asked the grizzled old man as Anna tried tactfully to shoo him out of the door.

"Nope. She won't be working here again, I'm afraid," Anna shook her head, grateful that this

Saturday shift had ground to a halt at last.

"Ooooo..." said Cat, padding through from the kitchen, her new shoes dangling by their ankle straps from her hands, and flopping down on the red vinyl of the window seat. "I'm in agony! How do you and Dorothy do it every day?"

Dorothy, busy wiping up the now empty tables, shot Anna a look.

We both wear shoes that aren't going to cripple us, Anna felt like saying.

"Did you see that old man?" said Cat, peering out of the window. "He tried to pinch my bum!"

"Really?" Anna replied, remembering watching Cat as she'd tried to take his order. Maybe the fact that she'd been merrily wrestling her pink bra into a more comfortable position while he'd been making up his mind had given him the wrong idea...

"Uhhhhh... I can't believe how tired I am," Cat yawned. "Still, I'll get home in time to veg out in front of the *Brookside* omnibus. Can I get my wages now? Or do I have to wait till Nick's back?"

It was on the tip of Anna's tongue to say that they still had an hour's worth of cleaning, tidying and setting up for tomorrow to do before they could knock off for the day. But one glance at Dorothy, who was vehemently shaking her head, put paid to that.

"You get off home, Cat," Anna assured her. "Me and Dorothy will lock up. And pop in tomorrow afternoon at closing time for your money, if that's all right."

"No problem," yawned Cat, her *Absolutely Fabulous* hairdo lurching precariously to one side. "See you tomorrow. It was fun, wasn't it?"

"Yep!" laughed Anna, holding the front door open as Cat clambered into her shoes again.

Fun, thought Anna, in a *red-hot-needles-poked-in-your-eyeballs kind of way...*

• • •

Ollie and the lads from The Loud were sprawled on the floor of *The Titanic's* tatty back-stage corridor, too despondent to care how grubby it was.

In a room off the corridor, they could hear the whooping and hollering of the Dungaree Brothers and their mates, celebrating their less than well-deserved win.

"Hey," said Dylan, coming along to join them and slithering down the greasy wall to their level. "Guess what? I was just talking to one of the other sound engineers and he said that the lead drongo in the boy band is – wait for this – *only* the nephew of that main judge, Kenny Whatsisface!"

"So *that's* why they won!" said Billy. "Well, it couldn't have been down to talent."

"Or costume design..." chipped in Andy.

"Anyway, who cares?" sniffed Joe. "This whole competition's been totally low-rent. I mean, this club's totally tacky for a start. And that record contract wasn't worth anything. The chance to record an album at 'Kenny's Studios' by the shopping centre and release it on 'Kenny's Kuts' record label? How corny is that? It's hardly Sony or Virgin, is it?"

Ollie said nothing. He simply looked hopelessly glum and stared morosely at the voucher The Loud had been presented with for coming second.

Dylan leant over and took a closer look at the wording on it.

"*This voucher gives a course of one month's unlimited relaxation treatments at all Kalifornia beauty salons...* I don't believe it – that's also owned by Kenny! Is this a stitch-up or what? So which one of you lucky guys gets to use this?"

Everyone except Ollie managed to raise a smile at Dylan's gentle sarcasm.

"What a waste of time..." Ollie muttered finally. "I was so sure that this was it! Oh, well, so much for stardom beckoning. It'll be back to normal in the caff tomorrow..."

"Except it won't," said Joe.

"What?" frowned Ollie.

"Uh, nothing," Joe shook his head.

"No, go on," Ollie pressed him.

"Well, it's not going to be normal, is it? Thanks to this stupid competition, hardly anyone's speaking to each other!"

"And that's *my* fault, is it?"

"Yes," said Joe defiantly. "You've just been charging along with this thing, not caring about what other people think, not even bothering to listen to what anyone else has got to say! It's like you don't even know what's going on in *my* life. You don't have a clue what I was doing yesterday and you don't have a clue what's been going on in my head either!"

The other lads were hardly breathing, they were so intent on this bust up breaking out between the two best mates.

"Are you trying to tell me something here, Joe?" said Ollie, his face white and pinched with hurt and anger. "'Cause it sounds like it! What's the deal – are you saying I don't listen to you? Go on then, surprise me! Tell me something I don't know!"

"OK, for your information, I passed my driving test yesterday – not that you'd be interested," Joe stated bitterly.

"Wow, Joe, I—" Ollie began, taken aback at his friend's news.

"But that's not my big news," shrugged Joe, his jaw clenching as he spoke. "Thing is, Ollie, I'm moving to London in September. And I'm leaving the band."

CHAPTER 21

APOLOGIES AND THANK YOUS

"So I'm sorry."

"No, *I'm* sorry!"

Kerry gazed earnestly across the Formica table at her friend, concerned and amazed that Maya had been going through all this worry over Alex without telling anyone.

"But I didn't really listen to *you*, Kez. I wasn't around so I didn't realise just how bad things had got between everyone in the crowd!"

"Well, hopefully, it's not going to be like that for much longer. After we got back home from the city last night, Ollie *promised* me that he's going to sort everything out, as from today, starting with Anna."

Both girls automatically glanced round to check for signs of any Ollie/Anna bonding as they both hurried about serving customers this busy Sunday morning.

"Probably hasn't had time yet," Maya reassured a fretting Kerry.

"So anyway," Kerry said, turning her attention back to Maya's concerns. "You definitely think there's something going on between Alex and this girl?"

"Well, yes. I mean, I was so sure he was holding stuff back from me that I just couldn't bear to see him last week; so I didn't turn up to photography club," Maya explained. "When he phoned to find out why, I pretended I didn't feel well. I said the same thing when he phoned on Thursday to see if we were going to the Railway Tavern. I said to him, 'I can't go, but why don't you? You can *always* take your friend Holly. *Again*'."

"What did he say?"

"Nothing – he just went quiet. That's why I know something's up."

"Didn't you see him this weekend?"

"No – he was away visiting his sister."

"Still, Alex and you are so cool together. I'm *sure* there can't be anything going on with him and that woman," said Kerry, who was sure of no such thing.

"Kez," Ollie interrupted, appearing suddenly at

their table. "Don't worry – I'm not bottling it. I will try and work things out. When I've got a sec..."

"I hope so..." whispered Kerry as he dashed away again.

• • •

"So do you feel better?" said Meg, taking a sip of her tea.

"I suppose," shrugged Joe, kicking his feet up on to the coffee table. "But it's not too brilliant, falling out with your best mate, and having him give you the silent treatment for the whole journey home."

"Mmm, I wish I could have come yesterday. Given you a bit of moral support."

"Don't worry, it wasn't a very nice atmosphere anyway."

"What, the competition or falling out with Ollie?" Meg gently teased him.

"Both!"

"Never mind. It's over now. And if Ollie reacted like that, it's probably just 'cause he's hurt – and it must be weird for him, thinking of you moving so far away after all the years you've known each other..."

"It'll be weird for me too, starting over, with no friends..."

"Ahem – apart from me!" Meg corrected him.

"Apart from you," smiled Joe. "At least you won't be far. Brighton's only an hour away, that's if poor students like us can afford the train fares back and forth!"

"But you'll have your—" Meg began then stopped herself.

"What?"

"Oh, nothing. I– I—"

Meg's momentary fluster was interrupted by a "Coooo-ee!" from the door; Joe's mum was back from popping out for the Sunday papers.

"*Joeyyyyy*!" she called. "Joe! Matt's here to see you!"

"Matt?" said Joe, squinting. "Bit early on a Sunday morning for him, isn't it?"

"Well, let's go and see what he wants then!" grinned Meg, reaching out and grabbing Joe's hand.

He was quite happy to be dragged anywhere by Meg, but Joe had to admit this was a little odd. It wasn't just the fact that Matt was up and about so early; why didn't he come straight in? Why was he hovering about outside? And why was his mother beaming at him as he went by, for all the world like she'd won the Lottery?

"Just a little something for you, Joey love," his mum's voice came from behind him as her son stood rocking on his heels on the doorstep.

The white Fiat had seen better days, that was for sure, but with the balloons tied round the aeriel and the thick red ribbon around the steering wheel, Joe was certain there was no other car he'd rather have.

"Like it?" grinned Matt. "Your mum asked me to help her choose it, so don't blame her if you hate it!"

"And don't worry, I didn't tie the balloons on very tight – so you don't have to drive around town with them all day!" giggled Meg.

"I– I– I love it. And I would happily drive around in it all day with the balloons tied on it. Aww, Mum... come here!" Joe managed to choke out, before enveloping Susie Gladwin in a big hug. "How can you afford it?"

"It's nothing much! It's only an old banger that me and Matt picked up at the garage down the road yesterday morning," she chirped, patting him fondly on the back. "Just my way of saying how proud I am of you: passing your driving test... dragging yourself to all your exams even though you were ill... and getting offered that place in London..."

Joe hugged her even tighter, profoundly grateful to have such a wonderful, understanding mum.

He hadn't even heard the phone ring.

"Sorry, I just picked that up," said Meg, interrupting the mother/son moment and pointing to the phone in the hall. "It was Ollie for you, Joe. He just asked if you could make it down to the End at closing time today. He says he needs your help..."

Joe blinked. It seemed like today was going to be full of surprises.

"Going down to that café again, hmm?" said Susie Gladwin. "Well, you're going to need these..."

Joe gave his mother a broad smile and grabbed the set of keys she was dangling in front of his nose.

CHAPTER 22

MAKING THINGS RIGHT

"It's *him*," said Sunny, barging into Maya's room without knocking.

"Oh," muttered Maya, knowing full well that her sister was talking about Alex.

Sighing she made her way out of her room and began padding down the stairs towards the phone. She glanced at her watch: it was 2.30 pm on Sunday afternoon. Alex must have got back early from his sister's and decided to call her straightaway. Not that Maya knew what she was going to say to him...

With three steps to go from the bottom, Maya froze.

Alex was standing in the hallway, gazing soulfully at her.

"Fancy a walk?" he asked, his eyes flicking imperceptibly towards Sunny, who'd followed Maya down the stairs like a stalking shadow.

"I'll get my jacket," she murmured, walking over to the coat rack.

• • •

"So you're right – I *did* go quiet when you suggested that I should take Holly out on Thursday. I was just a bit freaked out, since I'd just got in and listened to the message she'd left on my answering machine, pestering me to do exactly that!"

"But I don't understand," said Maya as they strolled through the park. "Why didn't you just tell me how she was acting?"

"I didn't want to tell you that stuff, not while you were all wrapped up in your exams!" Alex tried to explain. "I didn't think it would make you feel too happy, me saying, 'Oh, hey, Maya – I think my ex is coming on to me. She keeps phoning me up all the time and she's definitely been flirting with me!'"

"Well, I'd rather have had that than worry that you were hiding something!"

"OK, so I handled it wrong. But I was just thinking of you!"

Maya gazed up into his deep-set grey eyes. He was telling the truth, she could see that.

"Well," she smiled at him, reaching out for his hand, "I guess it's not *your* fault that women find you irresistible..."

"Urgh," groaned Alex, "but I don't *want* anyone finding me irresistible – it's too complicated! I just want you..."

"Good," said Maya. "Well, just keep that answering machine on then!"

"Yes, ma'am!" laughed Alex, saluting her. "So, come on, where would you like to go now we've got this sorted?"

"Actually, since you said that, you've reminded me of something," said Maya thoughtfully. "Can we go round to the café? Kerry said that Ollie's got something planned for closing time. He wants all of us in the crowd to be there. I think he's trying to do some sorting out too..."

• • •

As she stood waiting patiently for her customer to count out the money for his bill, Anna gazed dreamily over the top of the till and then did a quick double take.

When did they all arrive? she wondered, glancing over at the crowded window booth. Last time Anna had looked, only Matt, Joe and Meg were there. Now they'd been joined by Sonja, Andy and Cat... and Billy, with Maya and Alex too.

Her heart lifted – it had been ages since all the crowd had been together. And it was right about closing time; she could lock up after this customer and maybe sit down with everyone for five minutes before they left and she had to start cashing up. That would be lovely – Anna had missed all her friends so much lately.

But then her heart sank. There was no sign of Ollie – was he up to his skiving tricks yet again? Dorothy had said she would take care of the final tidying in the kitchen, so why wasn't Ollie out here wiping tables?

"Keep the change."

"Thanks," Anna smiled at the customer, following him to the door. "See you again!"

She flipped the 'closed' sign round on the door, but didn't slip the latch off yet. She still had the window table to gently move on...

"Sur-*PRISE*!!"

Anna nearly leapt out of her skin as she turned round and was bellowed at by everyone. She was even more surprised to see Ollie standing sheepishly by the counter, a ribbon-wrapped bottle in each outstretched hand and an envelope clenched between his teeth. Behind him, Dorothy stood in the doorway to the kitchen, beaming.

"Anna, I– *mumph*," mumbled Ollie, before awkwardly taking the card out of his mouth and starting again. "Anna, I have been a *total* pain in the—"

"Ollie!" Kerry yelped, censoring his language.

"Well, you know what kind of pain I've been, Anna," he shrugged with a laugh. "I just got carried away with all this band stuff—"

"And what a waste of time that was!" guffawed Billy good-naturedly from the sidelines.

"Exactly. Anyway, Anna, I'm so, so, *so* sorry – and just to show how sorry I am, I'd like to give you this – our prize from yesterday. Um, sorry about the teeth marks."

Everyone went quiet, waiting to see what Anna would say. She said nothing, only stretching forward to take the voucher out of his hand.

"I, well, all of us in The Loud thought that you could make better use of it than any of us. And I thought you could probably do with some relaxation sessions after what I've put you through recently!" Ollie smiled his lopsided smile, looking shy and adorable all at once.

Again, Anna said nothing. She raised her eyes from the voucher to the gift-wrapped wine in Ollie's hands.

"Oh, *these*," said Ollie, following her gaze and looking in turn at the bottles as if he'd forgotten he was holding them. "These are just from me – I thought we should all just celebrate being, y'know, together. They're not proper champagne or anything. I could only afford cheap fizzy stuff on the wages I get here—"

"Ollie," Anna interrupted him.

"Yes?" he said, blinking

Matt and the others held their breath.

"Call yourself a waiter?" Anna laughed, her eyes twinkling mischievously. "Where are the glasses then?"

"Woo-*hoo*!" yelped Ollie, instantly clattering one bottle down on the counter and priming his thumbs to pop the cork on the other.

As the fizzy stuff erupted in a cascade of froth, everyone leapt to their feet, scurrying over to help Dorothy, who was frantically passing out glasses.

"Feel like I haven't talked to you properly in ages," said Sonja, suddenly appearing next to Anna, her blue eyes wide and earnest.

"I feel the same," Anna smiled, passing her a full glass. "Let's catch up soon, yeah?"

"Yes, soon," Sonja smiled back warmly, before laughingly being bundled to one side by Billy as he attempted to claim his own glass of bubbly stuff.

"Heard Joe's news yet, Anna?" grinned Billy as Dorothy passed him some wine.

"No," Anna shook her head. "What's happening?"

She glanced over at Joe and Meg, who were clinking their glasses together.

"I'll let him tell you himself!" said Billy tantalisingly. "Bit of a bummer for The Loud, but it's brilliant for him – that's all I'm going to say!"

Anna bit her lip and wondered what was going on. But before she had a chance to go over to Joe, she felt someone grab her hand and squeeze it.

"I'm so pleased!" Dorothy whispered to her. "It's so lovely to see you and Ollie make up!"

"Thanks," smiled Anna, squeezing the older woman's hand back. "I was so worried about you and Irene saying you'd leave..."

"Ah, now – you didn't really fall for that one, did you?" winked the old lady. "As if Irene and I would ever do that to you..."

Anna opened her mouth and shut it again, suddenly realising she'd been duped. But it had worked. If Ollie hadn't apologised in the grand style he had, Anna had been all set to do it herself as soon as the café had closed.

"Hey!" came a deep, booming voice over the laughter and the radio that had been turned up. "There'd better be some of that left for me!"

Anna and the others turned to see Nick standing in the doorway, lightly tanned and sporting an Elvis T-shirt.

"So this is what happens when I go away for two weeks, is it? You lot have one long party..."

At the irony of that comment, Anna and Ollie exchanged wide-eyed glances. For a split second they stared at each other open-mouthed, then the giggles hit Ollie first, sending bubbles of fizzy wine shooting unexpectedly out of his nostrils.

"Ollie!" exclaimed Kerry, thumping her boyfriend's back in an effort to help him regain his composure.

But it was too late.

Ollie, Anna and now everyone but a puzzled Nick and a concerned Kerry were lost to fits of giggles...

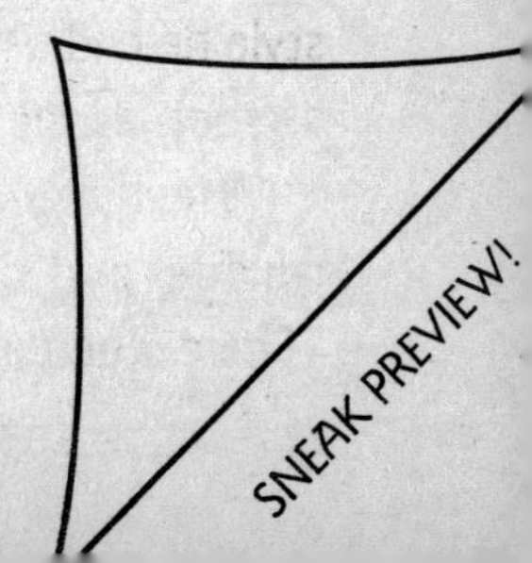

Sugar

SECRETS...

...& Confessions

SNEAK PREVIEW!

I can't believe how much I've messed up, Sonja thought angrily. *Everyone else is having a fabulous time because it's the end of exams and I should be too. As it is, I've got nothing to celebrate.* She stared at the unread magazine in front of her and wished she was anywhere but in the café right now.

Sonja suddenly felt stupid for coming here with the others. She had thought it might lift her spirits a bit, maybe take her mind off her problem. But now she was here and because it was obvious everyone else was in such a good mood, she wished she had stayed at home. In her room. Alone.

For the first time in her life Sonja felt she was drowning and it was a sensation that was completely alien to her. She had always been so sure about the path her life was going to take. Get good grades throughout school, go to university, get a First in Public Relations, get a good job with a flat and a nice car, have a career, a good time, loads of money, and a fab boyfriend (preferably Owen)...

The plan in her head had never deviated far from that – there was never anything else to consider, like flunking school or deciding to go off travelling, the sort of stuff that a lot of other people her age did.

Now, everything was different. The only certainty was that her plans were falling apart right before her eyes. She felt helpless to do anything to stop it. And doubly angry because of that.

"Hey, Son, why the long face?"

Matt interrupted Sonja's brooding with a friendly kiss on the cheek and his most winning smile.

"Uh, nothing to worry about, Matt, I'm just a bit tired, that's all. " Sonja found herself fiddling nervously with her magazine as she spoke, flicking through the pages without actually taking in what was on them.

"Great news about the band, isn't it?" he grinned, sliding into the seat beside her and putting an arm round her shoulder.

Sonja had a vague idea what he was talking about, though she hadn't listened to much of the conversation that had gone on earlier. "Er, yeah, fabulous," she said as lightly as possible. "Nice one."

"And I bet you're glad your exams are over now, aren't you?" continued Matt cheerfully. "It must be quite a relief not to have to wake up every morning worrying about what exam you've got today or how well you did in the last one. Not that you ever let them get on top of you – you're far too cool for that..."

If only you knew, Sonja thought bitterly.

"Hey, I've just had an idea," said Matt suddenly. "Why don't we all pile down to the festival and make a weekend of it? We could take a tent – my old man's got one in the garage somewhere – load up with sleeping bags... It'd be a right laugh. What d'you think?"

"Matt, that's about the best idea you've ever had," said Ollie in mock astonishment.

"It's the *only* idea he's ever had," quipped Cat.

"It is though, I love it, it's brilliant." Ollie was really animated now. He leapt up and down, his arms waving around like windmills. "We've got a massive tent somewhere at home too. I'm sure that between the two of them we could all squeeze in. It'll be great – a fantastic weekend away!"

"Well, I hope you guys have a great time. Send me a postcard, won't you?" Maya suddenly announced from the corner where she'd been sitting quietly.

"Oh, yes, *of course,*" said Kerry, looking sympathetically at Maya. "Your parents are going to love this one, aren't they?"

"Uh-huh." The tone was rueful. "They'll never let me go. Not in a million years..."

Order Form

To order direct from the publishers, just make a list of the titles you want and fill in the form below:

Name ....

Address ....

....

....

Send to: Dept 6, HarperCollins Publishers Ltd, Westerhill Road, Bishopbriggs, Glasgow G64 2QT.

Please enclose a cheque or postal order to the value of the cover price, plus:

UK & BFPO: Add £1.00 for the first book, and 25p per copy for each additional book ordered.

Overseas and Eire: Add £2.95 service charge. Books will be sent by surface mail but quotes for airmail despatch will be given on request.

A 24-hour telephone ordering service is available to Visa and Access card holders: 0141- 772 2281